# "Ultimately This Is About What's Best For Our Son."

To hear Nathan refer to Max as "our son" made Ana's heart twist. For a long time he had been just "her son." She wasn't sure if she was ready to give that up, to share him. But this wasn't about what she wanted. The only thing that mattered was what was best for Max.

"I guess a trial period would make sense," she told him. "Supervised visits of course."

"Of course," he agreed.

It meant having to spend time with Nathan, which she was sure would be heart-wrenching for her. Just having him in her home, remembering all the times they had spent there together, made her feel hollowed out inside. Alone. Since they split, she hadn't so much as looked at another man.

If a year and a half apart hadn't dissolved her feelings for Nathan, maybe she was destined to love him forever.

Dear Reader,

I must confess, I have a really hard time writing these letters. I can't help feeling a bit like a broken record. I find myself, over and over, going on about my characters, and how special they are. How unique and inspiring. But this time I thought I would try something different. I thought it might be fun to tell you about the character writing the characters.

Me.

So here goes. I'm a little shy when I'm in a group of people I don't know. I cannot function without my morning coffee—at least two cups. I hate to blog because I never know what to say. I am married to, hands down, the best husband ever. My children are the most talented and most brilliant in human history and ditto for my grandchildren. I used to love to sew and craft, but now I only have time to crochet. I am also an avid gardener when I can find the time. I am the youngest of three, and when my two older brothers weren't torturing me, they spoiled me rotten. I love animals, spring and poker night. I cannot play an instrument, or sing my way out of a paper bag, and my family always, *always* comes first.

So there you have it. Now, forget about me, and enjoy the book!

Best,

Michelle

# MICHELLE CELMER

## A CLANDESTINE CORPORATE AFFAIR

ISBN-13: 978-0-373-73119-0

A CLANDESTINE CORPORATE AFFAIR

Copyright © 2011 by Michelle Celmer

This edition published by arrangement with Harlequin Books S.A.

For questions and comments about the quality of this book please contact us at Customer_eCare@Harlequin.ca.

® and TM are trademarks of Harlequin Books S.A., used under license. Trademarks indicated with ® are registered in the United States Patent and Trademark Office, the Canadian Trade Marks Office and in other countries.

www.Harlequin.com

Printed in U.S.A.

**Books by Michelle Celmer**

Harlequin Desire

*Exposed: Her Undercover Millionaire* #2084
†*One Month with the Magnate* #2099
†*A Clandestine Corporate Affair* #2106

Silhouette Desire

*Playing by the Baby Rules* #1566
*The Seduction Request* #1626
*Bedroom Secrets* #1656
*Round-the-Clock Temptation* #1683
*House Calls* #1703
*The Millionaire's Pregnant Mistress* #1739
*The Secretary's Secret* #1774
*Best Man's Conquest* #1799
\*The King's Convenient Bride* #1876
\*The Illegitimate Prince's Baby* #1877
\*An Affair with the Princess* #1900
\*The Duke's Boardroom Affair* #1919
\*Royal Seducer* #1951
*The Oilman's Baby Bargain* #1970
\*Christmas with the Prince* #1979
*Money Man's Fiancée Negotiation* #2006
\*Virgin Princess, Tycoon's Temptation* #2026
\*Expectant Princess, Unexpected Affair* #2032
†*The Tycoon's Paternity Agenda* #2053

Harlequin Superromance

*Nanny Next Door* #1685

Silhouette Special Edition

*Accidentally Expecting* #1847

\*Royal Seductions
†Black Gold Billionaires

# MICHELLE CELMER

Bestselling author Michelle Celmer lives in southeastern Michigan with her husband, their three children, two dogs and two cats. When she's not writing or busy being a mom, you can find her in the garden or curled up with a romance novel. And if you twist her arm really hard, you can usually persuade her into a day of power shopping.

Michelle loves to hear from readers. Visit her website, www.michellecelmer.com, or write her at P.O. Box 300, Clawson, MI 48017.

To Jim, for being the best big brother
a pesky younger sister could ask for.

# One

Oh, this was not good.

Ana Birch glanced casually over her shoulder to the upper level of the country club deck, hoping to catch a glimpse of the man in the dark leather jacket, praying that she had been mistaken, that her eyes had been playing tricks on her. Maybe it just looked like him. For months after he dumped her she would see his features in every stranger's face. The dark, bedroom eyes and the sensual curve of his lips. She would see his broad shoulders and lean physique in men she passed on the street. Her breath would catch and her heart would beat faster…then sink miserably when she realized it was only someone who looked like him. In the eighteen months since he'd ended their affair, he hadn't so much as called her.

She finally caught sight of him standing by the bar, drink in hand, talking with one of the other guests. Her heart bottomed out, then climbed back up into her throat and lodged there. This was no illusion. It was definitely him.

*Oh, God.* How could Beth do this to her?

Hitching her nine-month-old son, Max, higher on her hip, she crossed the pristine, rolling green lawn, her heels sinking into the soft, spongy sod. *Note to self: never wear spiked heels to an outdoor kids' party. Or a silk jacket,* she added with annoyance, as Max wiggled and slid south again down her side.

In her skinny jeans and knee-high boots, with her freshly dyed, siren-red hair, she was the antithesis of the society mothers who drank and socialized while harried nannies chased their children. A fact that clearly escaped no one as curious glances followed in her wake. But no one dared insult the heiress to the Birch Energy empire, at least not to her face, which Ana found both a relief and an annoyance.

She spotted her cousin Beth standing by the gigantic, inflatable, plastic-ball-filled, germ-breeding monstrosity, watching her six-year-old daughter, Piper, the birthday girl, screaming and flailing inside with a dozen other children.

She loved Beth like a sister, but this time she had gone too far.

Beth saw them approaching and smiled. She didn't even have the decency to look guilty for what she had done, which didn't surprise Ana in the least. Beth's own life was so abysmally uneventful and boring, she seemed to take pleasure meddling in other people's business. But there was more at stake here than harmless gossip.

"Maxie!" Beth said holding out her arms. Max screeched excitedly and lunged for her, and Ana handed him over. Beth probably figured that Ana couldn't physically assault her while she was holding a baby.

"Why is *he* here?" Ana demanded under her breath.

"Who?" Beth asked, playing the innocent card, when she knew damned well *who*.

"*Nathan*."

Ana shot a look over her shoulder at Nathan Everette, chief brand officer of Western Oil, standing by the railing, drink in hand, looking as conservatively handsome and casually sophisticated as he had the day Beth had introduced them. He hadn't been Ana's type, as in: he had a successful career, and he didn't have tattoos or a police record. But he was a bigwig at Western Oil, so having a drink with him had been the ultimate "screw you" to her father. Then one drink became two, then three, and when he asked to drive her home she'd thought, what the heck, he's pretty harmless.

So much for that brilliant theory. When he kissed her at the door she'd practically burst into flames. Despite what she led people to believe, she wasn't the precocious sex kitten described in the social pages. She was very selective about who she slept with, and it was never on a first date, but she had practically dragged him inside. And though he might have looked conservative and even came off as a bit stuffy, the man definitely knew how to please a woman. Suddenly sex had taken on an entirely new meaning for her. Then it was no longer about defying her father. She just plain wanted Nathan.

Though it was only supposed to be one night, he kept calling and she found herself helpless to resist him. She was head over heels in love with him by the time he dumped her. Not to mention pregnant.

Nathan glanced her way and their eyes met and locked, and she found herself trapped in their piercing gaze. A cold chill raised the hair on her arms and the back of her neck. One that had nothing to do with the brisk December wind. Then her heart started to beat faster as that familiar awareness crept through her and heat climbed from her throat to the crest of her cheeks.

She tore her eyes away.

"He was Leo's college roommate," Beth said, tickling Max under the chin. "I couldn't not invite him. It would have been rude."

"You could have at least warned me."

"If I had, would you have come?"

"Of course not!" She'd spent the better part of the past eighteen months avoiding him. Having him this close to Max was a risk she simply could not take. Beth *knew* how she felt about this.

Beth's delicate brow pinched, and she lowered her voice to a harsh whisper. "Maybe I thought it was time you stopped hiding from him. The truth is bound to come out. Don't you think it's better now than later? Don't you think he has a right to know?"

As far as Ana was concerned, he could never know the truth. Besides, he'd made his feelings more than clear. Though he cared for her, he wasn't in the market for a committed relationship. He didn't have time. And even if he did, it wouldn't be with the daughter of a direct competitor. That would be the end of his career.

Wasn't that the story of her life. For her father, Walter Birch, owner of Birch Energy, reputation and appearances had always meant far more to him than his daughter's happiness. If he knew she'd had an affair with the CBO of Western Oil, and that man was the father of his grandson, he would see it as the ultimate betrayal. He had considered it a disgrace that she'd had a child out of wedlock, and he'd been so furious when she wouldn't reveal the father's name that he cut off all communication until Max was almost two months old. If it wasn't for the trust her mother had left her, she and Max would have been on the streets.

For years she had played by her father's rules. She'd done everything he asked of her, playing the role of his perfect little princess, hoping she could win his praise. She dressed in clothes he deemed proper and maintained a grade point average that would make most parents glow with pride, but not her father. Nothing she ever did was good enough, so when being a good girl got her nowhere, she became a bad girl instead. The negative reaction was better than no reaction at all. For a while, at least, but she'd grown weary of that game, too. The day she found out she was pregnant she knew for her baby's sake it was time to grow up. And despite his illegitimacy, Max had become the apple of his grandfather's eye. He was already making plans for Max to one day take over Birch Energy. If her father knew Nathan was Max's daddy, out of spite he would disown them both. How could she in good conscience deny her son his legacy?

That was, in part, why it was best for everyone if Nathan never knew the truth.

"I just want you to be happy," Beth said, handing Max, who had begun to fuss, back to her.

"I'm going to take Max home," Ana said, hoisting him up on her hip. She didn't think Nathan would approach her, not after all this time. Since their split he had never once tried to contact her. Not a phone call or an email, or even a lousy text. He'd gone cold turkey on her.

But running into him by accident wasn't a chance she was willing to take. Not that she thought he would want anything to do with his son. "I'll call you later," she told Beth.

She was about to turn when she heard the deep and unmistakeable rumble of Nathan's voice from behind her. "Hello, ladies."

Her pulse stalled then picked up triple time.

*Damn it.* Ana froze, her back to him, unsure of what to do. Should she run? Turn and face him? What if he looked at Max and just knew? But would running be too suspicious?

"Well, hello, Nathan," Beth said, air-kissing his cheek, giving Ana's arm a not-so-gentle tug. "I'm so glad you could make it. You remember my cousin, Ana Birch?"

Ana swallowed hard as she turned, tugging Max's woolen cap down to cover the small blond patch behind his left ear in his otherwise thick, dark hair. Hair just like his father. He also had the same dent in his left cheek when he smiled, the same soulful, liquid brown eyes.

"Hello, Nathan," she said, swallowing back her fear and guilt. *He didn't want you,* she reminded herself. *And he wouldn't have wanted the baby. You did the right thing.* He had to have heard about her pregnancy. It had been the topic of El Paso high society gossip for months. The fact that he'd never once questioned whether or not he was the father told her everything she'd needed to know.

He didn't *want* to know.

He looked exactly the same, not that she'd expected him to change much in a year and a half. And Nathan's cool assessment of her, the lack of affection and tenderness in his gaze, said she had been nothing more to him than a temporary distraction. A passing phase.

She wished she could say the same, but she missed him as much now, ached to feel that soul-deep connection that she'd never experienced with any other man, the feelings of love that had snuck up on her and dug in deep, and seemed to multiply tenfold every time he showed up at her door. Every fiber of her being screamed that he was the one, and she would have sacrificed anything to be with him. Her inheritance, her father's love—not that she believed for one second that Walter Birch loved anyone other than himself.

There wasn't a day that passed when she looked into her son's sweet face and didn't feel the sting of Nathan's rejection like a dagger through her heart. And now, the compulsion to throw herself in his arms and beg him to love her was nearly overwhelming.

Pathetic, that was what she was.

"How have you been?" he asked in a tone that was, at best, politely conversational, and he did little more than glance at her son. Hadn't he expressed quite emphatically that at this point in his career he didn't have time for a wife and kids? But she hadn't listened. She had been so sure that *she* was different, that he could love her. Right up until the moment he walked out the door.

She adopted the same polite tone, even though her insides were twisting with a grief that after all this time still cut her to the core. "Very well, and yourself?"

"Busy."

She didn't doubt that. The explosion at Western Oil had been big news. There had been pages of negative press and unfavorable television spots—courtesy of her father, of course. As chief brand officer, it was Nathan's responsibility to reinvent Western Oil's image.

"Well, if you'll excuse me," Beth said. "I have to see a man about a cake." Beth shot her a brief, commiserative smile before she scurried off, bailing on Ana when she needed her most.

She hoped Nathan would walk away too. Instead, he chose that moment to acknowledge her son, who was wiggling restlessly, eager for attention.

"This is your son?" he asked.

She nodded. "This is Max."

The hint of a smile softened his expression. "He's cute. He has your eyes."

Attention hound that he was, Max squealed and flailed his arms. Nathan reached out to take his tiny fist in his hand and Ana's knees went weak. Father and son, making contact for the first time...and hopefully the last. Sudden tears burned the corners of her eyes, and a sense of loss so sharp sliced through every one of her defenses. She needed to get out of here before she did something stupid, like blurt out the truth and turn a bad situation into a catastrophe.

She clutched Max closer to her, which he did not appreciate. He shrieked and squirmed, flailing his chubby little arms, knocking his wool cap off his head.

*Damn it!*

Before she could reach for it, Nathan crouched down and grabbed it from the grass. She cupped her hand around Max's head, hoping to cover his birthmark, but when Nathan handed her the hat, she had no choice but to let go. She angled her body so he wouldn't see the side of Max's head, but as she reached out to take the cap, Max shrieked and lunged for Nathan. He slipped against her silk jacket and she nearly lost her grip on him. Nathan's arms shot out to catch him just as she regained her grip and, heart hammering, she hugged Max to her chest.

"Strong little guy," Nathan said.

"He's high-spirited," she said, realizing too late that Max's left ear was in plain view. *Please don't let him notice.* She swiftly swung Max around and deposited him on the opposite hip. "Well, it was nice to see you again Nathan, but I was just leaving."

Without waiting for a reply she turned to walk away, but before she could take more than a step, Nathan's hand clamped down hard around her forearm. She felt it like a jolt of electricity.

"Ana?"

She cursed silently and turned to face him, and the second she saw his eyes she could tell that he knew. He had figured it out.

*Damn, damn, damn.*

That didn't mean she couldn't deny it. But not telling him and outright lying were two very different things. Besides, the birthmark was going to be tough to explain.

Oh, well, so what if he knew? He'd been quite firm that he didn't want children. He probably wouldn't even care if the baby was his, as long as she agreed never to tell anyone and never asked for his support. And why would she? Her trust fund kept her and Max living quite comfortably. Nathan could just go on with his life and pretend it never happened.

Nathan reached up and gently cupped her son's face, turning his head so he could see behind his ear. Thinking it was a game, Max batted at his hand and wiggled in her arms.

She'd heard of people going ghostly white but had never actually witnessed it until just then. He definitely knew, and he clearly wasn't expecting this. Hadn't even considered it being a remote possibility.

"A private word?" he asked, jaw tense, teeth gritted.

"Where?" They were at a party with at least two hundred other people, most of whom knew she and Nathan wouldn't have a lot to talk about. Where could they possibly go without drawing attention to themselves? "You wouldn't want to be seen with the daughter of a direct competitor," she snapped in a voice filled with so much pent-up resentment she barely recognized it as her own. "What would people think?"

Nathan's jaw tensed. "Just tell me this," he said under his breath. "Is he mine?"

Oh, boy. How many times had she imagined this moment? What she would say if ever faced with this situation. She had rehearsed the conversation a thousand times, but now that the moment was here her mind was totally blank.

"Answer me," he demanded, sounding far too much like her father.

*Did you really sneak a bottle of my good scotch into the school dance? Answer me, Ana Marie Birch!*

She had no choice but to tell Nathan the truth, but all she could manage was a stiff nod.

Nathan cursed, anger flashing in his eyes, holding her arm so tight he was cutting off the blood flow to her fingers. In all the time she'd been with him, she'd never seen him so much as raise his voice. His outrage was probably just a knee-jerk reaction. He was upset because she hadn't told him, but would ultimately be relieved when she assured him he had no responsibilities in regard to her son. Financial or parental. He might even thank her for being so reasonable and honoring his wishes. Then he would leave, and hopefully she would never have to see him again.

Of course there was another possibility. One she'd found too disturbing to consider until now. Or maybe she'd just refused to let herself go there. What if he wanted to be a part of Max's life? What if he wanted visitation and a say in the decisions? What if he tried to take Max away from her?

The thought made her clutch her son closer to her chest, which of course made him wiggle in protest. For nine months he had been her entire life. The only person who truly loved and needed her. She refused to let anyone, especially a man like Nathan, who didn't have time for a girlfriend much less a son, take that away from her.

"Should I assume," Nathan asked through gritted teeth, "that you never intended to tell me?"

"To be honest," she said, lifting her chin with a defiance that was meant to hide the fact that inside she was terrified, "I didn't think you would care."

# Two

He had a son.

Nathan could hardly wrap his mind around the concept. And Ana was wrong. He did care. Probably too much. The instant he saw her talking to Beth his heart slammed the wall of his chest so hard it stole his breath, and when their eyes met he'd experienced such a bone-deep need to be close to her, he was down the stairs and striding in her direction before he could consider the repercussions of his actions.

After he ended their affair, he must have picked up the phone a dozen times that first week, ready to tell her that he'd made a mistake, that he wanted her back, even though it would have been the end of his career at Western Oil. But he had worked too damned hard to get where he was to throw it all away for a relationship that was doomed from the start to fail. So he had done the only thing he could.

He'd gotten over her...or so he thought. Now he wasn't so sure.

She tried to jerk her arm from his grasp and her grimace said he was hurting her. *Damn it.* He released his grip and clamped a vice down on his temper. He worked damned hard to maintain control at all times. What was it about her that made him abandon all good sense?

"We need to talk," he said in a harsh whisper. *"Now."*

"This is hardly the place," she said.

She was right. If they disappeared together people were bound to notice. And talk.

"Okay, this is what we're going to do," he said. "You're going to say goodbye to Beth, get in your car and drive home. A few minutes after that I'm going to slip out. I'll meet you at your condo."

Her chin rose a notch. "And if I say no?"

She was trying to be tough, trying to play the spoiled heiress card, but he knew better. He knew that deep down the defiant confidence she flaunted like some badge of honor was nothing more than a smokescreen to hide the fact that she was as vulnerable and insecure as the next woman.

"Not advisable," he said. "Besides, you owe me the courtesy of an explanation."

Even she couldn't deny that, and after a brief pause she said, "Fine."

What else could she say? She may have been stubborn and, yes, a little spoiled, but she was an intelligent woman. She walked away, clutching her son—*their* son—unsteady on the grass in her ridiculously high-heeled boots. Hooker boots, his brother Jordan would have called them. Not the typical attire for an heiress, and even less appropriate for a mother, but she never had been one to play by the rules, which was what had drawn Nathan to her in the first place. Her confidence and her spunk had been an incredible turn-on, especially when he was used to dating "proper" women. The kind who would keep him grounded, who wouldn't tempt him from within the safe place he'd carved out for himself and back into the dark side. But she hadn't been nearly as wicked as she wanted people to believe. In fact, she'd coaxed him farther out into the light than any other woman had managed.

Nathan spotted Beth and headed in her direction. He didn't doubt for a second that she knew the baby was his. And the look on her face as he approached said she knew that he knew. "She swore us to secrecy," Beth said before he could get a word out.

"You should have told me."

She snorted. "Like you didn't already know."

"How could I have?"

"Come on, Nathan. You break up with a woman and a month later she turns up pregnant, and you're telling me you didn't even suspect it was yours?"

Of course he had. He kept waiting for a call from Ana. He trusted that if the child was his she would have the decency to tell him. When he didn't hear from her he just assumed the baby was another man's, which he'd taken to mean that she'd wasted no time moving on. Which he couldn't deny stung like hell.

Turned out there really hadn't been anyone else— at least, not that he knew of. That wasn't much of a consolation at this point.

"It was wrong of her to keep it from me," he told Beth.

"Yes, it was. But—and she would kill me if she knew I was telling you this—you broke her heart, Nathan. She was devastated when you ended the relationship. So, please, cut her a little slack."

That was no excuse to keep his child from him. "I have to go. Give the birthday girl a kiss for me."

Beth's brow cinched with worry. "Go easy on her, Nathan. You have no idea what she's been through the past year and a half. The pregnancy, the birth…she did everything on her own."

"That was her *choice*. At least she *had* one." Feeling angry and betrayed by people he trusted, Nathan turned and headed toward the parking lot. Although, honestly, what had he expected? He and Leo had drifted since their college days, and Beth was Ana's cousin. Had he really expected her to break the confidence of a family bond for a casual acquaintance? If that were the case, should Nathan have felt compelled in college to tell Beth how many times he had come back to the frat house to find her husband Leo, then her steady boyfriend, in his room with another girl?

Besides, he thought, as he slipped behind the wheel of his Porsche, maybe he had suspected the baby was his and deep down didn't want to know the truth. Maybe that's why he never called her, never confirmed for his own peace of mind. Maybe the truth scared the hell out of him. What would he do if it was his kid? What would he tell Adam Blair, his boss and CEO of Western Oil? He was having a child who just happened to be the grandson of the owner of the company's leading competitor. That would have been a disaster then, but now, since the explosion at the refinery, and the suspicion that Birch Energy might somehow be involved, it was a whole new ball game. Not only could he kiss goodbye any chance at the soon-to-be-open CEO position, he would probably lose the job he already had.

Besides, what the hell did he know about being a father, other than the fact that he didn't want to be anything like his own father? But the margin for error was still astronomical.

He'd been to Ana's condo in Raven Hill so many times he drove there on autopilot. When he pulled into the driveway, a white luxury SUV was already parked there. She must have traded in her sports car for something more practical. Because that was what responsible parents did. And despite everything, he didn't doubt for a second that Ana would be a good mother. She used to talk about losing her own mother and how her father ignored her. She said that when she had children they would be the center of her universe.

Nathan and his brother Jordan had the opposite problem. Their father had been on their backs, cramming his principles down their throats and bullying them into doing things his way since they were old enough to have free will. Which Nathan hadn't hesitated to exercise in full force, butting heads with the old man on a daily basis. Giving back as good as his father gave, until he'd pushed so far in the opposite direction, was so crippled by rage and indignation, he had lost a part of himself in the process.

He parked beside the SUV, let go of the steering wheel and flexed his fingers. He'd been gripping it so hard his arms ached. He needed to relax. Yes, he was pissed, but going in there half-cocked was only going to make a bad situation worse.

He took a deep, calming breath, got out, and walked to the porch. Ana was standing in the open doorway waiting for him, as she had been countless times before. They couldn't be seen in public together, so they'd spent most of their time together here. Only this time as she let him in and closed the door, she didn't slide her arms around his neck and pull him to her for a long, slow kiss. The kind that made the stress of the day roll off his shoulders, until nothing mattered but being with her. He wondered what she would do if he drew her against him and pressed his lips to hers.

She would probably deck him, and he would deserve it. But it was almost worth the risk. Despite the time that had passed, he wanted her as much now as the first day he met her. As much as the day he walked out the door. Cutting all ties, ending things before they both got in too deep, had been the kindest thing he could do for her. For either of them. And he'd be smart to remember that.

Ana had shed the silk jacket and boots, and in form-fitting jeans, a peasant blouse and bare feet, she looked more like a college student than someone's mother. As always, she was a total contrast to the conservative chinos and button-up shirt that was his standard uniform. His disguise, to hide the real man lurking underneath the spit and polish. He'd never admitted to anyone, not even Ana, how damned hard it could be to keep him contained.

He shrugged out of his jacket and hung it on the coat tree by the door. "Where's the baby?"

"He's in bed."

"I want to see him." He started for the hall that led to the bedrooms, but she stepped in his way.

"Maybe later."

Anger sparked, then ignited, hot and intense, and had his blood pumping through his veins. "Are you saying you refuse to let me see my own son?"

"He's asleep. Besides, I think it's best if we talk first."

He had half a mind to demand to see him, to push his way past her. Hadn't she kept him from the kid long enough? But she was standing there, arms crossed, wearing a mama-bear look that said it would be in his best interest not to screw with her or her child. When it came to their son, she clearly didn't mess around.

He clamped a vice down on his anger and said, "Okay, let's talk."

She gestured across the spacious living room to the couch. "Have a seat."

Her home had always had a relaxed feel, and despite the service that cleaned weekly there had always been clutter. But now, with toys strewn everywhere, it was like walking through a minefield to get to the couch. As he sat he had a vivid memory of the two of them sitting there together naked, her straddling him, head thrown back, eyes closed, riding him until they were both blind with ecstasy. The memory had his blood pumping through his veins again.

"Something to drink?" she asked.

How about a cold shower instead? "No thanks."

She sat cross-legged in the overstuffed chair across from him.

Since he saw no reason not to get right to the point, he asked, "So you thought it was okay to have my child and not tell me?"

"When you heard that I was pregnant, you could have asked," she said.

"I shouldn't have had to."

She shrugged, as if she saw nothing wrong with her actions. "Like I said, I didn't think you would care. In fact, I thought you would probably be happier not knowing. You made it pretty clear that you didn't want a family. If I had told you, what would you have done? Would you have risked your career to claim him?"

He honestly didn't know, which he couldn't argue legitimized her point. But this wasn't just about how it would affect his career. There were other factors to consider, things she didn't know about him. Still, he would have liked the opportunity to make that decision himself. "Either way it was my choice to make, not yours."

"If you didn't have time for me, how could you have time for a child?"

It wasn't just about not having time. She might not have understood it, she probably never would, but he did her a favor when he ended their affair. She made him drop his guard, lose control, and with a man like him that could only spell trouble. He just wasn't relationship material. Not the kind of relationship she needed anyway. The kind she *deserved*. She was too passionate and full of life. Too... sweet. She didn't need him dragging her down.

"What you really mean is," he said, "I hurt you, and this was your way to hurt me back?"

"That isn't what I said."

No, but he could see that he'd hit a nerve.

"This is getting us nowhere," she said. "If you want to talk about Max, fine. But if you came here to point fingers, you might as well leave."

He leaned forward. "You could at least have the decency, the *courage*, to admit you may have made a mistake."

"I did what I thought was best for my baby. For *everyone*." She paused, then added grudgingly, "But I won't deny that I was hurt and confused and maybe not considering everyone's feelings."

Nathan figured that was about as close to an admission of guilt, or an apology, as he was going to get. And she was right: pointing fingers would get them nowhere. Neither would flying off the handle. The only way to discuss this was calmly and rationally. And considering her tendency to leap to the defensive, he was going to have to be the sensible one. In short, he considered how his father would handle the situation, then did the exact opposite.

He swallowed his bitterness, and a fairly large chunk

of his pride, and said, "Let's forget about placing blame, or who wronged who, and why don't you tell me about my son."

"First, why don't you tell *me* what you plan to do now that you know about him," Ana said. There would be no point in him learning about a son he had no intention of seeing. Although he did seem to want to handle this in a civilized manner, and she was grateful. Though she could take whatever he could dish out and then some, it was always more fun not to be verbally drawn and quartered.

"To be honest, I'm not sure what I plan to do," he said. "I'm still trying to process this."

"You're worried about how it will affect your career?"

"Of course that's a concern."

"It shouldn't be. He's your son. You should love and accept him unconditionally. If you can't do that, there's no room in his life for you."

"That's a little harsh, don't you think?"

"No, I don't. He's my responsibility and I know what's best for him. And unless you're willing to claim him as your child, and carve out a permanent place in your life for him—and that includes regular visitation that is convenient for me—you can forget seeing him at all. He needs stability, not a sometimes father who yo-yos in and out of his life on a whim."

An uncharacteristic show of anger hardened his expression. "I imagine you'll be expecting child support as well," he said, jaw tense.

He just didn't get it. He thought she was being obtuse, but this wasn't about the money, or a need to manipulate him. This was all about Max and what *he* needed. "Keep your money. We don't need it."

"He's my child and my financial responsibility."

"You can't buy your way into his life, Nathan. He's not for sale. If you can't be there for him emotionally, for the long haul, you're out of the game. That's nonnegotiable."

She could see he wasn't thrilled with her direct approach, or her list of demands, but that was too damned bad. Parenting was tough, and either he was in or he was out. He couldn't do it halfway.

"I guess I have a lot to think about," Nathan said.

"I imagine you do." She rose from the chair, prompting him to do the same. "When you've made a decision, then you can see Max."

He pulled himself to his feet, looking irritated, and maybe a little shell-shocked. The enormity of what she was asking from him was not lost on her. Being responsible for another human being, knowing she would shape Max into the adult he would one day become, was terrifying and emotionally exhausting...and the most rewarding thing she had ever done or even imagined doing.

Until Nathan understood that and accepted it, he wouldn't get within fifty feet of Max.

"I need some time to think about this," Nathan said.

"I understand. And I want you to know that whatever you decide is okay with me. I would love for Max to know his father, but I don't want you to feel pressured into something you're not ready for. I can do this on my own."

He walked to the door and shrugged into his jacket, glancing down the hall to the bedrooms. For a second she thought he might ask to see him again, but he didn't. "Can I call you?" he asked.

"My number hasn't changed." He would know that if he had bothered to contact her in the past eighteen months.

He paused at the door, hand on the knob, and turned

back to her. "I am sorry for the way things worked out between us."

But not sorry enough to want her back in his life, she thought as he walked to his car.

She didn't doubt it was going to be a very long night for Nathan. Maybe even a long week, depending on how long it took him to make up his mind. He was not the kind of man to act on impulse. He thought things through carefully before making a decision of any kind. He once told her that their affair was the only spontaneous thing he'd done in his adult life. It had been a thrill to know that she'd had that kind of power over someone like him. Too bad she couldn't make him love her, too.

She watched out the front window until Nathan drove away, then she stepped outside and walked across the lawn to the unit next door, rubbing her arms against the cool air seeping through her sheer top. She knocked, and almost immediately Jenny Sorenson, her neighbor and good friend, opened the door, looking worried.

"Hey, is everything okay?" she asked, ushering Ana inside. Max was sitting on the living room floor with Portia, Jenny's fifteen-month-old daughter. Ana hadn't been sure how Nathan would react, so she'd felt it was wisest to keep Max out of the picture.

"Everything is fine. I'm sorry to dump Max on you like that without an explanation, but I didn't have a lot of time."

When Max heard her voice he squealed and crawled in her direction, but then he got distracted by the toy Portia was banging against the coffee table and changed course. Max was an independent kid, and unless he was wet, hungry or hurt, toys took precedence over Mom any day.

"You looked really upset when you dropped him off. I was worried."

"I ran into Max's dad today. He may or may not be back in the picture. He wanted to talk, and I felt it would be best if Max wasn't there." She hadn't told Jenny the details of the situation with Nathan. In fact, up until the time Ana had Max, she and Jenny, a conservative and soft-spoken doctor's wife, had barely said hello. Then one afternoon when Max was a few weeks old and suffering a pretty nasty case of colic, Jenny heard his screams through the open window and stopped by to offer her help. Like Ana, she'd also made the choice to raise her baby without the help of a nanny or an au pair, and she'd been a godsend. She taught Ana a few tricks she'd learned with her own colicky baby, and they had been friends ever since. Still, Ana was selective about what she did and didn't tell her.

"How do you feel about that?" Jenny asked her.

"Conflicted. I'd love for Max to know his father, but at the same time I feel as though I'm setting him up to be let down. If he's even half as bad as my father—"

"It's only fair to give him a chance," Jenny said firmly, glancing at her daughter, who was in a tug-of-war with Max over a stuffed bear. "A baby needs its father."

Even though Portia barely ever saw hers. Brice Sorenson, a busy surgeon, was often out of the house before the baby woke, and home after she was tucked in bed. If they were lucky, they might see him for a few hours Sunday between hospital rounds and golf. Though Jenny hadn't come right out and said it, it sounded as though even when he was home, he wasn't really there. He was older than Jenny, and had grown children from a first marriage. He didn't change diapers or clean up messes, and he'd never once taken a midnight feeding. The scenario struck a familiar and troubling chord for Ana. One she refused to accept for Max.

"The ball is in his court now," Ana told Jenny. And if Nathan wanted any less than what was best for Max, she would cut him out of his son's life without batting an eyelash.

# Three

Though Nathan hated that Ana's words made so much sense, after several days of considering his son's well-being, he knew she was right. Either he was in or he was out of Max's life. There was no doing it halfway. But he had to consider how claiming his son could impact his career. He was sure that if the truth came out he could kiss his chances at the CEO spot goodbye. The board would see it as a direct and flagrant conflict of interest. Since they learned that the explosion at the refinery was the result of someone tampering with the equipment, people had been quick to point the finger at Birch Energy—even though as of yet they hadn't been able to prove any sort of connection.

But even more important, how would his being in the kid's life influence Max? Nathan had no idea what it took to be a father—at least, not a good one. The only thing he knew for sure was that he didn't want to be anything like his own father: accepting nothing but perfection, verbally, and sometimes physically, lashing out if anyone dared fall short of his unrealistic expectations.

Nathan was too much like his old man, too filled with suppressed anger to ignore the possibility that he would be a terrible father. Yet he couldn't just forget that there was a child out there whom he'd brought into this world, who shared half of his genetic code. He had to at least try. And if he couldn't be there for Max, even though Ana said they didn't need his money, Nathan would see that Max was taken care of financially for the rest of his life.

He called Ana Wednesday afternoon and asked if he could come by to talk.

"How about eight-thirty tonight? After Max goes to bed."

"You still won't let me see him?"

"Not until I've heard what you have to say."

Fair enough. "I'll see you at eight-thirty then."

"See you then."

He hung up just as Emilio, the company CFO, knocked on his office door.

Nathan gestured him in, thinking that this visit had something to do with the new marketing budget his department had submitted Monday morning. If Western Oil was going to rebuild their reputation with the public, it was going to cost them.

Instead, Emilio said, "Sorry to interrupt," and handed him a small white envelope. "I just wanted to drop this off."

"What is it?"

"An invitation."

"For...?"

"My wedding."

Nathan laughed, thinking that either he'd misheard or it had to be a joke. "Your *what*?"

A grin kicked up the corner of Emilio's mouth. "You heard me."

Nathan knew no one more vehemently against marriage than Emilio. What the hell had happened?

Curiosity getting the best of him, he tore the envelope open and pulled out the invitation, his mouth dropping open when he recognized the bride's name. "This wouldn't be the Isabelle Winthrop who was indicted for financial fraud?"

"Apparently you haven't been watching the news. All charges against her were dropped last Friday."

That explained it. He'd worked late Friday then went to the party Saturday, and since then pretty much all he'd thought about was Ana and his son. He couldn't recall turning on the television or even picking up a newspaper. "And now you're marrying her?"

"Yep."

Nathan shook his head. "Didn't her husband die just a few months ago?"

"It's a long story," Emilio said.

*I'll bet it is,* he thought. One he was surprised he hadn't heard about before now. But like himself, Emilio was a very private person. And Nathan couldn't be happier that he'd found someone he wanted to be with for the rest of his life. "One I can't wait to hear," he said.

Emilio grinned. "By the way, I looked over your proposal. I'd like to set up a meeting with Adam to go over the numbers. Probably early next week."

"Have your secretary call my secretary."

Nathan spent the rest of the afternoon in meetings, during the last of which they ordered in dinner, which saved him the trouble of having to go out or pick up carryout to eat at home before he changed out of his suit and left for Ana's place. He arrived at eight-thirty on the nose. Sometime since Saturday she had decorated the front of her condo for the coming holiday. Lighted balsam and fir swags framed the door and windows, and she'd hung a wreath decorated with Christmas bulbs and fresh holly on the front door. Nathan hadn't hung a single decoration in his high-rise apartment downtown. He didn't even own any. Why decorate for the holidays when he was never there? If he decorated anywhere, logically it should be his office, since that was where he spent the majority of his time.

Before he could knock on the door it swung open.

"Right on time," Ana said. She was dressed in hot pink sweatpants and a matching hoodie over a faded T-shirt stained with something orange that may or may not have been mashed-up carrots. Her fiery red hair was pulled haphazardly back with a clip, and she didn't have any makeup on. Yet she still managed to look sexy as hell.

Motherhood looked damned good on her.

She stepped aside to let him in. "Excuse the mess, but I just got Max settled, and I haven't had time to straighten up yet."

She wasn't kidding. It looked as if a bomb had gone off in the living room. He had no idea one kid could play with so many toys.

"It looks like there were a dozen kids here," he said, shrugging out of his jacket and hanging it on the coat tree.

"Five, actually. It's playdate day, and it was my week to host."

"Playdate?"

"You know, a bunch of parents get together with their kids and let them play together. Although me and my next-door neighbor, Jenny, are the only actual parents. Two others are nannies, and one is a French au pair. Jenny and I are both pretty sure the au pair is sleeping with the baby's father. And one of the nannies told us that the couple she works for is on the verge of divorce, and he sleeps in the spare bedroom now."

He had no idea playdates could be so scandalous.

"Isn't Max a little young to be playing with other kids?" he asked.

"It's never too early to start socializing children."

Proving that he knew absolutely nothing about parenting. "You don't have a nanny?"

"I love being with Max, and I'm in a position where I don't have to work now. I like being a stay-at-home mom. Not that it's been easy, but well worth it."

His mother had been too busy with her charities and her various groups to take much time for her sons.

Ana gestured into the living room. "Come on in and have a seat. Would you like something to drink?"

He could probably use one. Or five. But no amount of alcohol was going to make this easier. "No thanks."

She waited until he sat on the couch, then took a seat on the edge of the chair. "So, you've made a decision?"

"I have." He propped his elbows on his knees, rubbing his palms together. Ana watched him expectantly. He wasn't sure how she was going to like this. She was probably expecting a definitive answer, but he wasn't ready to give her that. Not yet. "I'd like to have a trial period."

Her brows rose. "A *trial* period? This is not a gym membership we're talking about, Nathan. He's a baby. A human being."

"Which is exactly why I think jumping into this would be a bad idea. I know nothing about being a parent. As you pointed out, I never planned to have a family. For all I know I might be a lousy father. I'd like the opportunity to try it out for a few weeks, spend some time with Max and see how he takes to me."

"Max is nine months old. He loves everyone."

"Okay then, I want to see how *I* take to *him*."

"And if you don't...*take to him?* What then?"

"I'll honor your wishes and remove myself from Max's life completely."

She shook her head. "I don't know..."

"I know you were hoping for a more definitive answer, but I honestly think this is the best way to do this. And it's not a decision I came to lightly. I just..." He sighed, shook his head. "I don't know if I'm ready for this. I've made a lot of mistakes in my life, Ana, and this is too important to screw up."

"I'm assuming there's also the question of how this will go over at work."

"I won't deny that was a factor in my decision. Our current CEO is leaving, and I'm one of the select few who are competing for the position. I don't want to rock the boat."

"So it *is* about work," she said, not bothering to hide the bitterness in her voice.

"I have to consider everything," he said. "But ultimately this is about what's best for our son."

To hear Nathan refer to Max as "our son" made Ana's heart twist. For a long time he was just "her son." She wasn't sure if she was ready to give that up, to share him. But this wasn't about what she wanted. The only thing that mattered was what was best for Max.

Her knee-jerk reaction was to say no way, either he was in or out; but in all fairness, she'd had almost nine months to get used to the idea of being a parent. He'd had a child thrust on him without warning, and now he was expected to make a decision that would impact his and their son's life forever. And hers. Could she honestly blame him for erring on the side of caution? He had clearly given this a lot of thought and seemed to have Max's best interest in mind. Wasn't that what really mattered? Not to mention that Nathan had shown vulnerability, which she knew had to be tough for him. He was a successful and well-respected man. Admitting he might not be able to hack it as a father couldn't have been easy for him. She commended him for his honesty.

"I guess a trial period would make sense," she told him. "Supervised visits, of course."

"Of course," he agreed.

Which meant having to spend time with Nathan, which she was sure would be heart-wrenching for her. Just having him in her home, remembering all the times they had spent there together, made her feel hollowed out inside. Alone. Since they split, she hadn't so much as looked at another man. Not that she'd had a whole lot of time for dating these days, but she had gone out with friends a few times, attended social functions with her father. Men had tried to strike up conversations, asked her to dance, but she just wasn't interested.

If a year and a half apart hadn't dissolved her feelings for Nathan, maybe she was destined to love him forever. Or maybe being around him again would make her realize that he wasn't as wonderful as she used to think. The man was bound to have flaws. Little character traits that annoyed her. Maybe all this time she'd been building him up in her mind, making him into something he really wasn't.

A renewed sense of hope filled her. Maybe this would turn out to be a good thing for her. But they had to be cautious.

"I also think it would be best if no one knew about this," she said.

He looked relieved, probably because he was worried

about his position at Western Oil. But there was more to it than that.

"I think that's a good idea," he said.

"We'll have to be really careful. These things have a way of blowing up, and that could be devastating for Max."

"He's a baby. It's not as if he can pick up a newspaper."

"Not yet. But someday he will. If you decide, for whatever reason, that you can't be a part of his life, I don't want him to know about you. If your identity gets out now, you can bet he'll hear about it eventually. Besides, my father adores Max, but if he were to learn that you're the father, he would know that our affair was just another way of defying him. He would disown me and Max on principle."

"Still trying to win his affection?"

"I don't give a damn what he thinks about me, but Max has a future at Birch Energy, if he should so decide that's what he wants to do. Right now it's his legacy. It doesn't seem fair to deny him that for my own selfish reasons."

"Yet if I decide to be a part of his life you risk that very thing."

"Because knowing his real father is too important. He needs a male influence in his life, and as it stands, my father is the best I can do. And who knows, maybe Max isn't destined to fail him. With me, he never seemed to get over the fact that I wasn't the son he'd always wanted."

"So, is that really all I was to you?" he asked. "Just another way to defy your father?"

At first. Until he wasn't anymore. Until she fell stupidly and hopelessly in love with him. But that would have to remain her little secret. Her pride depended on it. "Does that come as such a shock?"

"Not really, considering we both know it isn't true."

And what about him? Did he get off on making women

fall for him, then breaking their hearts? Was it all just a game to him? And how was she supposed to react to his accusation? If she denied it, she would look as though she were hiding something. If she admitted the truth…well, that wasn't even an option.

She refused to give him the satisfaction of any response.

"So, what days would be best for you to see Max?" she asked him. "His bedtime is eight, so if you want to do weeknights it will have to be before that. Sunday afternoons would work too."

"Weekdays will be tough. I've been swamped at work. I'm lucky if I can get out by nine most nights."

"No one said it was going to be easy. You have to make priorities."

His look said he was poised to jump to the defensive, but instead he took a deep breath and said, "If I go into the office early tomorrow, I could be out of there by six-thirty. That would get me here a little before seven."

"That's a start," she said.

"Tomorrow it is then."

A long, uncomfortable silence followed, where neither seemed to know what to say next. Or maybe they had said all there was to say.

"Well, I guess since that's settled…" He rose from the couch.

"It's been a long day, and I don't know about you, but I could go for a glass of wine." She knew the second the words left her mouth it was a bad idea, but she just wasn't ready for him to leave.

*You can't force him to love you*, she reminded herself. And she wouldn't want to. She wanted someone without the relationship hang-ups, who loved her unconditionally. If that kind of man even existed.

Nathan studied her, one brow slightly raised. "Are you asking me to stay?"

Yeah, bad idea. "You know what, forget it. I don't think—"

"Red or white?"

His question stopped her. "Huh?"

"The wine. Do you have red or white?" The hint of a smile tugged at his lips. "Because I'm partial to red."

She shouldn't be doing this. She was still vulnerable. She was only setting herself up to be hurt. For all she knew he could be involved with someone else now. Maybe that was part of the reason for the trial period.

*Character flaws,* she reminded herself. She couldn't find them if she didn't spend at least a little time with the man.

Just this once, and after this, she would see him only if Max was there.

"Then you're in luck," she told him. "Because I have both."

# Four

"If you're sure it's no trouble," Nathan said, a part of him hoping she would say it was.

"No trouble."

She walked to the kitchen and he sat back down. He wasn't sure what the hell he thought he was doing. He came here to discuss his son, and now that they had, he had no reason to stay. The problem was, he didn't *want* to leave.

Maybe it was time to admit what deep down he had known all along. He still had unresolved feelings regarding his relationship with Ana. Despite what she probably believed, ending it hadn't been easy for him, either. Ana was the only woman who had ever made him feel like a whole person. Like he didn't have to hide. Almost… normal. But he knew that eventually his demons would get the best of him—they always did—and she would see the kind of man that he really was. Knowing Ana, and the kind of woman she was, she would want to try to fix him.

Well, it wouldn't work. He wasn't fixable. And the less time he spent with her, the better. Especially in situations where Max wasn't there to act as a buffer. So why wasn't he stopping her as she walked to the kitchen and pulled two wineglasses down from the cupboard? Why didn't he get up, grab his coat and get the hell out?

Damned if he knew. Although he was sure good old-fashioned stupidity played a major part.

"So," she said from the kitchen. "You said you're up for the CEO position?"

He turned to face her. She was standing at the counter opening a bottle of red wine. "It's between me, the CFO Emilio Suarez and my brother Jordan."

"Your brother, huh? That must be dicey." The cork popped free and she poured the wine. "If I recall correctly, your relationship has always been...complicated."

"Is that the polite way of saying he's an arrogant jerk?"

"I actually met him at a fundraiser last year," Ana said, carrying the two glasses into the room.

"Did he hit on you?"

"Why? Are you jealous?" She handed him one, their fingertips touching as he took it from her. It was an innocent, meaningless brush of skin, but boy, did he *feel* it. Way more than he should have. If she noticed or felt it, too, she wasn't letting on. She sat back down in the chair, curling her legs beneath her, looking young and hip and sexy as hell. And yes, maybe a little tired.

"I ask," he said, "because Jordan hits on all beautiful women. He can't help himself."

"I believe he was there with a date."

Nathan shrugged. "That's never stopped him before."

"No, he didn't hit on me. Although maybe it had something to do with the fact that I was eight months pregnant and as big as a house."

"Somehow I can't see that stopping him either."

She laughed. "Come on, he's not *that* bad."

He didn't used to be. When they were growing up, Nathan had been his brother's protector. He couldn't begin to count how many times, when they were kids, that he had taken the blame for things his brother had done to shelter him from their father's wrath, or stepped between Jordan and their father's fists. As the older brother he felt it was his responsibility to shelter Jordan, who was quiet and sensitive. A *sissy,* their father used to call him. But instead of the loyalty and gratitude Nathan would have expected, Jordan learned to be a master manipulator, always pointing the finger at Nathan for his own misdeeds. At home, in school. He became the golden child who could do no wrong, and Nathan had been labeled the troublemaker. Not that Nathan hadn't gotten into enough trouble all on his own. But after all these years it still chapped his hide.

"Jordan is Jordan," Nathan said. "He won't ever change."

"When will the new CEO be announced?" Ana asked.

Not until the investigation into the explosion at Western Oil was complete, but he couldn't tell her that. Only a select few even knew there *was* an investigation. The explosion was caused by faulty equipment—equipment that had just been checked and rechecked for safety—and as a result thirteen men were injured. The board was convinced it had been an inside job, and they suspected that Birch Energy—specifically Ana's father—was behind it. The goal was to flush out whoever was responsible. But it had been a slow, arduous and frustrating process.

"We haven't been given a definitive date," he told Ana. "A few more months at least."

"And how will you feel if it goes to Jordan?"

"It won't." Of the three candidates, in his opinion, Jordan was the least qualified, and Nathan was sure that the board would agree. Jordan used charm to get where he was now, but that would only take him so far.

"You sound pretty sure about that."

"That's because I am. And no offense, but I don't want to talk about my brother."

"Okay. What do you want to talk about?"

"Maybe you could tell me a little about my son."

"Actually, I can do better than that." Ana set her wine down, got up from her chair and walked to the bookcase across the room. She pulled a large book down from the shelf and carried it over. He expected her to hand it to him; instead she sat down beside him. So close that their thighs were almost touching.

He liked it better when she was across the room.

"What's this?" he asked.

She set the book in her lap and opened it to the first page. "Max's baby book. It has pictures and notes and every milestone he's reached up until now. I've been working on it since before he was born."

Clearly she had, as the first few pages consisted of photos of her in different stages of her pregnancy, and even a shot of the home pregnancy stick that said "pregnant" in the indicator window. And her earlier self-description that she was "as big as a house" in her eighth month was obviously a gross exaggeration. Other than looking like she had swallowed a basketball, her body appeared largely unchanged.

"You looked good," he said.

"I was pretty sick the first trimester, but after that I felt great."

The next page was sonogram photos—with one that clearly showed the baby was a boy—and notes she'd taken after her doctor visits. The pages that followed were all Max. And damn, maybe Nathan was partial, but he sure was a cute baby. But as Ana sat beside him slowly turning the pages, he caught himself looking at her instead. The familiar line of her jaw and the sensual curve of her lips. The soft wisps of hair that had escaped the clip and brushed her cheek. Eighteen months ago he wouldn't have thought twice about reaching up to tuck it back behind her ear. To caress her cheek, stroke the column of her neck. Press his lips to the delicate ridge of her collar bone…

Damn. He would have thought that over time his desire for her would have faded, but the urge to put his hands on her was as strong as ever. And for her sake as much as his own, he couldn't.

"He's a cute kid," he said, as she reached the end of the book and flipped it closed. "He actually looks a lot like Jordan did at that age."

She got up and carried the book back to the shelf, sliding it in place. A part of him hoped she would return to the conch and sit beside him, and the disappointment he felt when she didn't was a clear indication that he needed to get the hell out of there. He should be concentrating on his son, but all he could think about was her.

He swallowed the last of his wine and pulled himself to his feet. "It's late," he said, even though it was barely past nine. "I have an early morning. I should get going."

If his leaving disappointed her, she didn't let on. She followed him as he walked to the door. "So, we'll see you tomorrow around seven?" she asked.

"Or sooner if I can manage it." He shrugged into his jacket and she opened the door. This would normally be the part where she slid her arms up around his neck and kissed him goodbye, and usually tried to talk him into staying the night. God knows he had been tempted, every single time, but that was always where he drew the line. Sleeping over insinuated a level of intimacy where he never dared tread. Otherwise women got the wrong idea. Especially women like Ana.

"I'm glad you came over tonight," she said.

He stopped just shy of the threshold. "Me, too."

"And I meant what I said before, about the choice you make. Even after this, if you decide you can't do this, I won't hold it against you. Being a parent is tough. It takes a *ton* of sacrifice."

"It sounds almost as if you're trying to dissuade me."

"It's also the most rewarding experience I've ever had. It changes you in a way you would never expect. Things I used to think were so important just don't seem that critical anymore. It's all about him now."

He wasn't sure if he was ready to make a child the center of his life. He wouldn't even begin to know how. "Now you're scaring the hell out of me."

She smiled. "I know it sounds daunting, and it is in a way. It's tough to explain. You'll either feel it or you won't, I guess."

Or maybe it was a chick thing, because he'd never heard any of his friends with kids describe it that way.

"I guess we'll just have to wait and see," he said.

"I guess."

He had the distinct feeling she wanted to say something else, so he waited a beat, and when she didn't he turned to walk out. He was one step onto the porch when she grabbed his arm.

"Nathan, wait."

He turned back to her. If she was smart, she wouldn't touch him, but the damage was already done. Now all he could think about was pulling her into his arms and holding her, pressing his lips to hers.

"When we were sitting there looking at Max's baby

book," she said, "it made me realize how much he's changed in the past nine months."

He wasn't sure what she was getting at. "Isn't that what kids are supposed to do?"

"Of course. I just…I guess it made me realize how much of his life you've missed already. I just wanted to say…I wanted you to know that…" She struggled with the words. "I'm…sorry."

Wow. An actual apology. And his surprise must have shown, because she swiftly added, "I still contend that everything I did was in Max's best interest."

"So…you're *not* sorry."

"I did it in Max's best interest, but that doesn't mean it wasn't a mistake."

Maybe there was something wrong with him, but seeing her so humbled was a major turn-on. And the way she was holding his arm, standing too close, was pushing the boundaries of his control.

He leaned in slightly, just to test the waters, to see what her reaction would be. Her eyes widened a fraction and her breath caught. He was sure she would retreat, but instead her pupils dilated and her tongue darted out to wet her lip.

Holy hell.

Not exactly the reaction he'd been hoping for. Or was it? He could be realistic, or he could be smart about this. Realistically, if he leaned in and kissed her, she would kiss him back, and though it might take one night, or five nights, they would wind up back in bed together.

The smart thing to do would be to back off now while he still could, and that was exactly what he planned to do. But it wasn't easy. "I should go."

She nodded, looking slightly dazed. "Okay."

He looked down at her hand and said, "Unless you're coming with me, you're going to have to let go."

"Sorry." She blinked and jerked her hand away, and by the glow of the porch light he could swear he saw her blush. Ana was not the blushing type. She was utterly confident and without shame—on the outside anyway. He couldn't decide who was more arousing, the unflappable vixen or the vulnerable girl.

So he stepped away. "See you tomorrow."

She nodded. "See you tomorrow."

He started down the steps, then stopped just as she was closing the door. "Hey, Ana."

"Yeah?"

"By the way, apology accepted." Then he turned and walked to his car.

Ana closed the door and leaned against it. *Oh my God.* He had almost kissed her. He had leaned in, his eyes on her mouth…

The idea of his lips on hers again made her heart beat faster and her breath quicken. And as wrong as she knew it was, she would have let him. As if she wasn't feeling confused and conflicted enough already.

Sitting there with Nathan, going through Max's baby book, she got to thinking about how precious each and every minute with her son had been. The idea that she had deprived Nathan of that and, even worse deprived Max of the chance to know his daddy, made her feel selfish and thoughtless. What gave her the right? Max's well-being? Well, suppose it hadn't been good for him? What if she had done more harm than good? What if Max grew up with a hole in his life, in his soul?

She hated that Nathan was making her second-guess herself, that she couldn't trust her instincts. Then there was that "apology accepted" remark. What was up with that? Did he mean it, or was he just playing some angle? Did he have ulterior motives? If she were him, she wouldn't be so quick to let her off the hook.

*You're giving him too much power,* she warned herself.

Not just that, but what in God's name had possessed her to touch him? She hadn't done it consciously. Until he'd asked her to let go, she hadn't even realized her hand was on his arm. She wanted to find his flaws, but not in bed. Besides, she knew for a fact that sexually, he was about as perfect as a man could be. So perfect that it made her blind to everything else. As evidenced by the fact that when he dumped her it seemed to come out of the clear blue with no warning. They hadn't even had so much as a disagreement. As far as she knew, everything was fantastic, them *bam,* it was over. Apparently there had been some problem that she wasn't seeing.

All the more reason not to sleep with him.

Her cell phone rang, and she pulled it out of her pocket to check the display, half-hoping it was Nathan calling to cancel for tomorrow. It was Beth. Ana was supposed to call her when Nathan left, but apparently Beth was impatient.

"Is he gone yet?" she said when Ana answered.

"He left a few minutes ago."

"So, what did he decide? Does he want to be Max's daddy?" Beth had been convinced from the time Ana learned she was pregnant that Nathan would want the baby and would slip easily into the role of being a father. She obviously didn't know Nathan as well as she thought she did.

"He wants a trial period."

*"What?"* she shrieked. "What the heck for?"

"Lots of reasons. But the gist of it is that he wants what's best for Max."

"Max needs his father. *That's* what's best for him."

"Well, Nathan doesn't see it that way. He's not convinced

he'll be a good father. And he's concerned about the reaction at work."

"So, are you going to let him do it?" she asked.

"What else can I do? I can't force him to want to be Max's daddy."

"But he *is* Max's daddy. He needs to be there for his son."

"I get the feeling there's more to it than he's letting on. He said something about having made mistakes in the past."

"What kind of mistakes?"

"I'm not sure. It was very cryptic. I thought maybe you would know what he was talking about. Maybe something that happened in college?"

"Nothing comes to mind. The only major mistake I've seen him make is leaving you."

She twisted the lock, engaged the deadbolt then switched off the porch light. "I think he almost kissed me."

Beth made a sound of indignation. "Are you serious?"

"Yeah." She walked into the living room and grabbed the two empty wineglasses. "We were at the front door saying goodbye and he was looking at me."

"Looking, or *looking?*"

*"Looking."* She carried the glasses into the kitchen and set them next to the sink. "Then he *leaned.*"

"He's got a lot of nerve. Does he think having a kid together is an open invitation back into your pants?"

Yeah, about that...she grabbed the bottle of wine and poured herself a second glass. "I sort of...touched him."

*"What?* Where?"

"His arm. Actually, just the sleeve of his jacket."

"Oh." Beth sounded disappointed, like maybe she thought it would be something more scandalous, like his fly.

Ana took a sip of wine, noticing the lip balm mark on the empty glass. That must be her glass, meaning she was drinking out of Nathan's glass. The idea of putting her lips on the rim where his had been sent a warm shiver down her spine.

Ugh! She was hopeless. She dumped it down the sink and set the glass down.

"I probably shouldn't have invited him to stay for a glass of wine either," she told Beth.

"Maybe this is a stupid question, but did you *want* him to kiss you?"

*"No."* She paused, then blew out a frustrated breath. "And *yes*. I still have all these feelings for him. But damn it, he already eviscerated my heart once. I would be a moron to go back for seconds."

"You know I'll stand by whatever you decide to do, hon, and this probably goes without saying, but be careful. Don't jump into anything without thinking it through first. Okay?"

"I won't, I promise." At least, she would try. "The problem is, when I'm close to him, it's like my brain ceases to function. Like…animal magnetism or something. It's been that way since the day I met him."

"When are you going to see him again?"

"He's stopping over to see Max tomorrow evening around seven."

"And Max goes to bed at eight-thirty?"

"Yeah, why?"

"Well, if something was going to happen, it would be after that, right?"

"I suppose."

"Then why don't I call you around eight forty-five. That way if you need moral support, I can talk some sense into you."

She hated to think that she would be that weak, but why take chances? "I think that sounds like a pretty good idea."

"You're tough, Ana. You can do this."

Beth was right. She had been through worse things than this, so why, right now, wasn't she feeling so tough?

# Five

Any time Ana had spent worrying that Max and Nathan might not bond had been a big fat waste.

Max adored Nathan. He'd been utterly fascinated with him since the second Nathan walked in the door, and spending the last two hours watching them play had flat out been the most heartwarming, confusing and terrifying experience of Ana's life.

For someone who had so little experience with babies, Nathan did everything right. He was gentle and patient, but not afraid to play with Max, who was used to—not to mention lived for—roughhousing with the older kids in the playgroup. "He's all boy, isn't he?" Nathan said, his voice full of pride as he swung Max up over his head, making him squeal. He didn't even seem to mind when Max smashed gluey bits of partially chewed zwieback into his designer shirt, or spilled juice from his sippy cup on Nathan's slacks.

Nathan was a complete natural with Max. So much so that Ana couldn't help feeling a bit like the odd man out. Max was so focussed on Nathan, she had ceased to exist. She was actually a little relieved when it was time to put Max to bed. At least she would get a few quality moments with him when she tucked him in, but then Nathan asked if he could help get Max ready for bed. Since the day he came home from the hospital, Max's bedtime was a ritual that had always been just the two of them. She knew she was completely unjustified in feeling that Nathan was overstepping his bounds. After all, they were *supposed* to be getting to know one another. Still, she couldn't help feeling a little jealous. Especially when she got Max changed and into his pajamas, and it was Nathan he reached for to put him into bed. That was tough.

"What should I do now?" Nathan asked her.

"Just lay him in bed and cover him up." She gave Max a kiss, then watched from across the room as Nathan lay Max, a little awkwardly, into bed, then pulled the blanket up over him.

"Good night, Max," he said, smiling down at him with the same dimpled grin Max was giving him, and though Ana was *dying* to walk over to the crib, if only to make sure he was covered and safely tucked in, to kiss him one more time and tell him she loved him, she knew she had to let father and son have this time together.

She'd just had no idea this would be so damned hard.

"Is that it?" Nathan asked.

She nodded and switched off the lamp on his dresser. "He'll go right to sleep."

Nathan followed her out of the bedroom and into the living room. Things had gone really well tonight, so why was she on the verge of an emotional meltdown? Why the tears brimming in her eyes?

She was being stupid, that was why. Max was still her baby, still depended on her for everything, and no one could take that from her. Having a daddy in his life didn't mean Max would love her any less.

"Well," Nathan said, "he's a great kid."

"He is," she agreed, hoping he didn't hear the hitch in her voice. She walked to the kitchen to load the dinner dishes into the dishwasher, hoping Nathan would take the hint and leave. Instead he followed her.

"That seemed to go well," he said, leaning against the counter beside the stove while she stood at the sink, her back to him.

"Really well," she agreed, blinking back the tears pooling in her eyes. *Stop it, Ana, you're being ridiculous.* Was she PMSing or something? She never got this emotional. She was tougher than this.

He was quiet for a minute then asked, "Ana, is something wrong?"

"Of course not," she said, the squeak in her voice undeniable that time, as was the tear that spilled over onto her cheek. My God, she was acting like a big baby. She had learned a long time ago that crying would get her nowhere. Her father had no tolerance for emotional displays.

Nathan laid a hand on her shoulder, which only made her feel worse. "Did I do something wrong?"

She shook her head. The apprehension in Nathan's voice made her feel like a jerk. He was genuinely concerned, and he deserved an explanation. She just didn't know what to tell him. Not without sounding like a dope.

"Ana, talk to me." He turned her so she was facing him. "Are you crying?"

"No," she said, swiping at the tears with her shirtsleeve. As if denying it would make her tears any less real.

"I'm confused. I thought it went okay tonight."

"It did."

"So…why the tears? Are you having second thoughts about this?"

She shook her head. "It's not that."

"Then what is it? Why are you so upset?"

She bit her lip, looked down at the floor.

He put his hands on her shoulders. "Ana, we can't do this if you don't talk to me."

*Please don't touch me*, she thought. It only made it worse.

"If I did something wrong—"

"No! You did everything right. Max adored you. It couldn't have gone more perfect."

"And you think that's a *bad* thing?"

"No. Not exactly."

Nathan's brow furrowed with confusion. Of course he was confused. She wasn't making any sense.

"Since the day Max was born it's just been the two of us. He depends on me for everything. But tonight, seeing you two together—" Her voice cracked. *Damn it Ana, hold it together.* "I guess I was jealous. I don't know what I would do if Max didn't need me anymore."

"Of course he needs you."

She shrugged, her shoulders heavy under the weight of his hands, and more of those stupid tears spilled over.

He cursed under his breath, then slid his arms around her and pulled her against him. And, oh God, it was so good. To hell with being strong. She wanted this. She'd wanted it for *so* long. She locked her arms around him and held on, feeling as if she never wanted to let go again. He would have to pry her loose, peel her away from him. She closed her eyes and breathed him in, rubbed her cheek against the solid warmth of his chest. He was so familiar, and perfect.

God, she was pathetic. She wasn't even trying to resist him. And Nathan wasn't making this any easier. Instead of pushing her away, he was holding on just as tightly.

"I think I'm just a novelty," he said. "A new toy to play with."

It took her a second to realize that he was talking about Max. "No, he really loved you, Nathan. It's almost as if he sensed who you were." She gazed up at him. "And that's good. That's the way it should be. It's what I want. I'm just acting stupid."

"I'm sure what you're feeling is totally normal."

He could have the decency to act like a jerk. To tell her she was being irrational and stupid. Instead of being a tool, and making her hate him, he was doing everything right. Where were those flaws she was supposed to be finding?

"You really need to stop being so nice to me," she said.

A grin tipped up the corner of his mouth. "Why?"

"Because you're making it impossible for me to hate you."

"Maybe I don't want you to hate me."

She had to. It was her only defense.

The house phone rang, and she realized that it must be Beth, calling to stop her from doing something stupid.

Too late.

She slid her arms up Nathan's chest and around his neck, pulled his head down to her level and kissed him, and there wasn't even a millisecond of hesitation on his part. Everything in her said, *Yes!* She blocked out the ringing of the phone, and the whisper of her own nagging doubts, and concentrated on the softness of his lips, the taste of his mouth, the burn of his beard stubble against her chin. Good Lord, did the man know how to kiss. He was tender, yet demanding. It was addictive, like a drug, and all she could think was *more.* Her body ached for his touch.

Nathan's big hands tightened around her hips, and suddenly her feet were off the floor. Her butt landed on the hard surface of the countertop, and her legs instinctively wrapped around his waist.

*Closer.* She wanted to be closer to him. Needed to feel her breasts crushed against the hard wall of his chest. Nathan cupped her behind and tugged her against him, trapping the stiff ridge of his erection against her stomach. He slid his hands upward, under the hem of her shirt, and his warm palms settled against her bare waist.

*Naked.* They needed to be naked, right now. She wanted to feel his skin, the hard ridges of muscle that used to be as familiar to her as her own body. She clawed at the tails of his shirt, tugging them free from his pants, and Nathan must have had the same thing in mind, because he was sliding her shirt up...

The doorbell rang, followed by frantic pounding. *What the hell?*

Nathan broke the kiss and backed away. "I think someone is here."

No, no, no. This wasn't fair. Maybe if they ignored it, the person would go away. They stood motionless, waiting. Then the bell rang again, followed by more pounding. At this rate, whoever it was, they were going to wake Max.

"I had better go see who it is," she told Nathan. So she could *kill* them.

She straightened her top and darted for the door just as the phone started to ring again. This had better be damned important. She yanked the door open to find Beth standing on her porch, hand poised to knock again, cell phone to her ear. As soon as she snapped her phone closed, the house phone stopped ringing.

"Hi!" she said brightly, muscling her way past Ana into

the foyer. "I was in the neighborhood, so I thought I would stop by."

In the neighborhood? At eight forty-five on a weeknight? Beth lived twenty minutes away. From the frantic knocking she was obviously a woman on a mission, and Ana knew exactly what that mission had to be.

Beth looked past Ana and her eyes widened almost imperceptibly.

Ana turned to see Nathan walking to the door, his tails retucked, clothes neat. To look at him, no one would guess that he'd been about to jump her bones.

"Hello, Beth," he said.

"Hi, Nathan. I didn't realize you were here."

Like hell she didn't, and Ana could see Nathan's bullshit meter zip into the red zone.

"My car in the driveway didn't tip you off?" he asked.

"Oh, is that *your* car?" She cut a look Ana's way. "I hope I haven't come at a bad time."

That was exactly what she was hoping.

"Actually, I was just leaving," Nathan said, grabbing his jacket from the coat tree.

Damn it! "Beth, would you excuse us for just a second?"

"Of course," Beth said, shooting her a look that said, *Don't try anything funny.*

Ana followed Nathan onto the porch, shutting the door behind her. "You don't have to go. I can get rid of her."

"Is that really what you want?"

Her first instinct was a big fat yes, but something made her pause and consider what he was asking. Was it what she wanted? Thirty seconds ago she was one hundred percent sure. But now that she'd had a minute to calm down, to think rationally, she had to wonder if she was making a mistake. She would sleep with him, and then what? Have another brief affair that would end in a month or so with her heart sliced and diced again? Was that worth a few weeks of really fantastic sex? If he decided to keep seeing Max, she would be stuck with him for a very long time. At least until Max was eighteen. And weren't things uncomfortable enough already?

"I think we both know that it would only complicate things," he said, and her heart took a steep dive.

She knew a brush-off when she heard one. What he really meant to say was, *he* didn't want *her*. Hadn't she been the one to start it this time? He had probably only hugged her for comfort, not to seduce her, but she had taken the ball and run with it. He could have stopped her, but after that awful emotional display of hers, maybe he was afraid of hurting her feelings. What could be more embarrassing? Or horrifying?

"You're right," she said, folding her arms against a sudden gust of cool air. Or maybe that chill was her heart turning to ice.

"Are we still okay for Sunday?" he asked.

"Of course. What time is good for you?"

"Why don't I come by around noon? I'll bring lunch."

That had quite the "family" ring to it. The three of them having lunch and spending the afternoon together. But she didn't want to discourage him, not when he and Max had gotten along so well tonight. Because this was about Max, not her. "Um, sure. That would be great."

"Great. I'll see you Sunday." He stepped off the porch into the darkness, and though she was tempted to stand there and watch him go, she had Beth to deal with. She stepped back inside but Beth wasn't waiting by the door.

She found her in the kitchen pouring a glass of wine. "Rough day?"

"It's not for me," Beth said, corking the bottle and

putting it back in the fridge. Then she held the glass out for Ana. "It's for you. You look like you need it."

She did. She took the glass from Beth. "I take it you weren't just *in the neighborhood*."

"Let's just say I had a hunch that a phone call wasn't going to cut it. Too easy to ignore if you're otherwise occupied. Besides, I've always preferred the direct approach."

Ana took a swallow of wine then set the glass on the counter. "Good idea."

"If I hadn't shown up, you would have slept with him, wouldn't you?"

She had been two seconds from dragging him to her bedroom. Or hell, they may have done it right there on the kitchen counter. It wouldn't have been the first time.

Her look must have said it all, because Beth folded her arms, cocked one hip and said, "Forget Max. *You're* the one who needs supervised visits."

"No, because it's not going to happen again. We just decided that it would complicate things too much."

"He says that now—"

"No, he means it. I think that was just his polite way of saying he's not interested."

Beth's brow furrowed. "Then why put the moves on you?"

"He didn't."

Beth looked confused, then her eyes went wide. "*You* seduced *him?*"

"I tried." Ana shrugged. "I guess that lean the other day wasn't a *lean* after all."

And the hug had been nothing more than a friendly gesture. He didn't want her eighteen months ago, and he didn't want her now.

"Oh, sweetie," Beth said, pulling her into her arms for a hug. She was getting that a lot today.

"I'm so stupid."

"No you're not." She held Ana at arm's length. "He's the stupid one for letting you go in the first place. He doesn't deserve you."

"Yet I still love him." She wished she could turn her feelings off like a spigot, the way her father did. She wished that she were stronger. And she wished this wouldn't hurt so much. "I'm pathetic."

"You just want to be happy, and you want your son to have what you missed out on. A complete, cohesive family. There's nothing pathetic about that."

Max might never have a mommy and daddy who loved each other, but it was possible that he would at least have two parents who loved him. If that was the best she could do for her son, she could live with that.

# Six

Nathan sat in his office Tuesday afternoon, browsing on his phone the photos Ana had emailed him of his visit Sunday. Though he had spent a couple hours with Max Thursday, and nearly the entire day at Ana's on Sunday, it didn't really hit home the bond that had begun to form between him and Max until he saw pictures of the two of them together. He hadn't realized how alike they looked. Not just features, but expressions and mannerisms. And he hadn't noticed the adoration in Max's eyes when he gazed up at him. The kid was really taking to him, and Nathan couldn't deny the tug of parental affection.

Ana, on the other hand, seemed as though she could take Nathan or leave him. He had hoped they might get a chance to talk about what had happened Thursday night, but she'd made herself pretty scarce. Other than snapping a few pictures, she'd spent most of her time in the spare bedroom with her scrapbooking paraphernalia, updating

Max's baby book. A few times when he did try to start a conversation she'd given him the brush-off. Apparently she'd had no trouble whatsoever forgetting that kiss.

He had known that hugging her was probably a bad idea, that he was tempting fate, but she had looked so confused and miserable that he hadn't been able to stop himself. He knew the instant her body was pressed to his, and her arms wrapped around him, that he had to kiss her, but then she'd slipped her arms around his neck and kissed him first. If Beth hadn't shown up, he didn't doubt for a second that they would have wound up in bed together. And it would have been a huge mistake, because as he suspected at the time, Ana was only reacting to the highly emotional situation. When he gave her an out, she gladly took it.

Oh, well, easy come, easy go.

He wasn't sure what kind of game she was playing with him. He just wished he could shut his feelings off so easily.

Nathan tried to get himself invited to stay for dinner Sunday, but Ana wasn't biting. She said they had plans for the evening, although she didn't say what they were. He had hoped they could have a quiet family dinner, he could tuck Max into bed again, then he and Ana could relax with a glass of wine and talk. He had forgotten until recently how much he enjoyed spending time with her. He left her condo at four-thirty wondering what was more disappointing: not being with Max, or not being with her.

Since the instant Beth had introduced Nathan and Ana he had been drawn to her. And while it was true that their relationship had begun based on little more than sex—and really fantastic sex at that—he found what he missed most about her were the times they just talked. She had a very unique and quirky way of looking at the world. Despite her station in Texas society, there were no pretensions, no ego. She was who she was, and when he was with her, he almost felt he could be who he was, too. That she was the kind of woman who would accept him. But accepting him, and deserving him, were two very different things. But damn, had he missed her when it was over.

It would never work for them, so why was he sitting here devising plans to spend more time with her? Things like leaving work early and showing up at her door unannounced with dinner tonight.

There was a knock at his office door, and he looked up to see his brother let himself in. "Hey, what's up?"

"Did Mom call you?"

"When I was in a meeting. I haven't had a chance to call her back. Why, is something wrong?"

"No. She wants you to bring the wine this year."

"The wine?"

Jordan laughed. "For Christmas dinner. It's a week from this Saturday."

"Seriously?" Nathan looked at his desk calendar. It seemed as though just a week ago it was Thanksgiving. And frankly, dinner with his mother once a year was more than adequate. "Maybe I'll have the flu this year."

"If I have to go, so do you."

"I have an idea. How about neither of us goes?"

"She's our mother."

"She gave birth to us. The nanny was our mother. Maybe we should go have dinner with her."

"It's *Christmas*," Jordan said. "The time for forgiveness."

He sighed and leaned back in his chair. "Fine. I'll call her and let her know."

"Should we get her a gift?"

Nathan folded his arms. "How about a plaque that says *Mother of the Year*?"

"Funny."

He might consider it if he thought for a second that she would appreciate the gesture. But when a twelve-year-old kid spent a month's worth of allowances to get his mother a necklace for her birthday, only to find it crammed down into the garbage the next day, it left a lasting impression.

"Isn't it enough that I'm spending an entire evening with her?"

"It's not going to bother you if I get her something?"

"Not in the least."

"So," Jordan said offhandedly. "Anything new with the investigation?"

Nothing Nathan could tell him. Though Adam and the board had promised to keep Jordan in the loop in regard to the investigation, he needed plausible deniability. Jordan was operations officer and worked closely with the men in the refinery. They respected and trusted Jordan. If they knew there were agency operatives working undercover among them and thought that Jordan was a part of it, that respect and trust would be lost. That was too important to sacrifice, especially now.

Besides, as of the last report that had landed on Nathan's desk, the agency hadn't made any progress in the investigation and was no closer to learning who tampered with the equipment. And Jordan had seemed particularly antsy to get results lately. He valued each and every man at the refinery, and he didn't want to believe that someone he trusted could be responsible for the explosion.

"Nothing new," he told his brother.

"If there were, would you tell me?"

He didn't answer.

Jordan shook his head. "That's what I figured."

If he thought for a second that he could trust his brother, he would tell him the truth, but Jordan would only take the information and use it to benefit himself. Everything was a competition to him. He was convinced that was why Jordan fought for the CEO position at Western Oil. It was some sort of twisted sibling rivalry.

"Anything else?" Nathan asked him.

"Nope, that's it," Jordan said, then added on his way out the door, "Don't forget to call Mom."

He should probably do that now before he forgot. Hopefully he could make it quick. He picked up the phone and dialed his mother's place and the housekeeper answered. "Your mother is with her bridge club, Mr. Everette. You can try her cell."

"Could you just let her know that I got her message and I'll bring the wine for Christmas dinner?"

"Of course, sir."

After he hung up, he sat back in his chair and considered all the work he should get done this afternoon, and weighed it against spending time with Max and Ana. They won, hands down.

He shut down his computer, got up and grabbed his overcoat. His secretary, Lynn, looked up as he walked past, clearly surprised to see him in his coat.

"I'm taking off early today. Would you please cancel my appointments for the rest of the day?"

Her brow furrowed with worry. "Is everything okay?"

It was pretty sad to know that he was so chained to his job, he couldn't leave work early without his secretary thinking something was wrong. "Fine. I just have a few personal things I need to take care of. I'll be in early tomorrow. Call me if anything urgent comes up."

He ran into Adam, the CEO, on the way to the elevator.

Adam looked at his watch. "Did I fall asleep at my desk? Is it after eight already?"

Nathan grinned. "I'm leaving early. Personal time."

"Everything okay?"

"Just a few things I need to take care of. By the way, how is Katie?" Adam's wife, Katie, lived two hours away in Peckins, Texas, a small farming community, where she and Adam were currently building a house and awaiting the birth of their first baby.

"She's great. Getting huge already."

Nathan was sure the long-distance relationship had to be tough, but Adam's beaming grin said they were making it work. Nathan wondered what it would be like to be that happy, that content as a family man. Unfortunately, he would never know.

"She's actually in town this week," Adam said. "She was thinking of having a small holiday gathering this Saturday. Just a few people from work and a couple of friends. I don't suppose you could make it."

He had been hoping to spend Saturday evening with Ana and Max, but with the CEO position in the balance, now wasn't a good time to be turning down invitations from the boss. "I'll check my schedule and let you know."

"It's last-minute, I know. Try to make it if you can."

"I will."

Nathan was stopped two more times on his way to the elevator, then he was corralled into the coffee shop in the building lobby briefly before he finally made it out the door and to his car. He stopped at home to change, noting as he stepped in the door the absolute lack of anything even remotely festive. He didn't even bother to display the Christmas cards that had been arriving in a steady stream the past couple of weeks. He never decorated for the holidays. He didn't have the time or, truthfully, the inclination. Most of his Christmas memories were the kind better off forgotten.

When he bought this place five years ago he'd had it professionally decorated, mainly because he didn't have time to do it himself. It was aesthetically pleasing, but it had no heart. He'd never put his own stamp on it. He spent so little time there, he might as well be living in a hotel. In contrast, Ana's condo, despite being a mess most of the time, was a home. When they were dating he'd spent most of his free time there instead of bringing her back to his place. The truth was, he never brought women home.

Recalling the stains on his slacks the last two times he visited Max, this time Nathan opted for jeans and a polo shirt. He was out the door by four, and pulled in Ana's driveway beside her SUV at four-ten. A gust of cold northern wind whipped around him as he walked to the porch. He knocked on her door, hoping she wouldn't be angry with him for stopping by unannounced.

She pulled the door open, Max on her hip, clearly surprised to see him. "Nathan, what are you…" She trailed off, looking him up and down, taking in his windblown hair, his casual clothes. "Whoa. That *is* you, right?"

Ana may have been confused, but Max wasn't. He squealed with delight and lunged for Nathan. Ana had no choice but to hand him over.

"Hey, buddy," Nathan said, kissing his cheek, and he told Ana, "I got out early today, so I thought I would come by and see what you're doing."

She stepped back so he could bring Max out of the brisk wind and shut the door behind them. She was dressed in a pair of skinny jeans and a sweatshirt, her feet were bare and her hair was pulled back into a ponytail. Damn, she was pretty. The desire to pull her into his arms and kiss her hello was as strong now as it had been a year and a half ago.

"You got out *early?*" she said. "I thought you were swamped."

He shrugged. "So I'll go in early tomorrow."

"But we don't have a visit scheduled."

"I wanted to see Max. I guess I missed him. I thought I would take a chance and see if you weren't busy."

"Oh." She looked as though she wasn't quite sure what to make of that. "We sort of have plans. We were going to have an early dinner then go get a Christmas tree."

"Sounds like fun," he said, more or less inviting himself.

"You hate the holidays," she said.

"Who told you that?"

"*You* did."

Had he? "Well, then, maybe it's time someone changed my mind." He paused, then said, "Is that Thai place you used to love so much still around?"

She folded her arms, eyeing him skeptically. "Maybe."

"We could order in. My treat."

The hint of a grin pulling at the corner of her mouth said she was close to caving. "Well, I suppose if I'm going to get a free meal out of it…"

He grinned and handed Max over to her so he could take off his coat.

Ana sat on the couch, listening to the all-holiday music channel on the satellite radio, watching as Nathan set up the Christmas tree in the stand.

This was probably a really bad idea. She probably shouldn't have invited Nathan to come tree hunting with them. The more she saw of him, the harder it was to keep her feelings in check, but Max had been so happy to see him, and Nathan had seemed pretty darned happy to see him, too. She just hadn't had the heart to turn him away. Besides, getting a Christmas tree was supposed to be a family activity. Not that she and Max and Nathan were a family. Not in the conventional sense, anyway. And Max was so little it wasn't as if he would remember it.

So, was she doing this for Max, or for herself?

Good question.

Max had fallen asleep in the car on the way home and had gone straight to bed, so there was really no reason for Nathan to be here. She was perfectly capable of setting the tree up by herself. So why, when he offered to do it, had she said yes? Why wasn't she telling him to go?

Because she was pathetic, that's why. Because spending the afternoon with him, and going to pick out a tree together, had been everything she could have imagined it would be. Because she wanted them to be a family, wanted it so badly she was no longer thinking rationally.

She'd been doing her best to avoid Nathan, to give him and Max time to get to know one another, but it seemed as though the less she talked to him, the more he tried to talk to her. She was all for them being friends, but her feelings were still a bit raw. They were going to have to set some rules about his popping in unannounced. Especially if he decided to be a permanent part of Max's life, which certainly seemed to be the way he was leaning. She hadn't brought it up yet. She figured he would broach the subject when he was ready.

"So, what do you think?" Nathan asked, stepping back to admire his work. "Is it straight?"

"It's perfect." The tree was larger than she usually got, but she'd figured what the heck, it was only for a few weeks, and she knew Max would be so excited when he woke up and saw it in the morning. Tomorrow night, after the branches had time to settle, they would decorate it. Everything about this holiday season would be special because it was Max's first.

Nathan grabbed his hot chocolate from the credenza where he'd set it and sat down on the couch beside her, resting his arm across the cushion behind her head. And he was sitting so that their thighs were nearly touching. What was this? A first date? Did he have to sit so close? There was a perfectly good chair across the room. Why didn't he sit there? Or even better, why didn't he leave? Would it be rude to ask him to go?

With the fireplace lit, and only the lamp by the couch on, there was an undeniable "date" vibe in the air. Or maybe she was mistaking intimate for cozy. Cozy and *platonic*.

"I had fun tonight," he said, sounding surprised by the realization.

"Does that mean you're changing your opinion about the holidays?"

"Maybe. It's a start at least."

"Well then, maybe I should let you help us decorate the tree tomorrow."

Ugh! Did she really just say that? What was *wrong* with her? It was as if her brain was working independently from her mouth. Or maybe it was the other way around.

Nathan grinned. "I may just take you up on that."

Of course he would. She was supposed to be avoiding him, not manufacturing family activities that Max would be too young to remember anyway. She was only making this harder on herself.

"What was it you disliked so much about Christmas anyway?" she asked him.

"Let's just say it was never what you would call a heartwarming family experience."

"You know, in all the time I've known you, you never once talked about your mom and dad," she said. "I take it there's a reason for that. I mean, if they were awesome parents I probably would have heard about it, right?"

"Probably," he agreed. Then nothing.

If she wanted to know more, obviously she would have to drag it out of him. "So, are they still together?"

"Divorced." Nathan leaned forward to set his cup down on the coffee table. "Why the sudden interest in my parents?"

She shrugged. "I don't know, I guess it would be nice to know about the family of the father of my baby. Especially if he's going to be spending time with them."

"He won't be."

"Why not?"

"My mother is an elitist snob and my father is an overbearing bully. I see her two or three times a year, and I haven't talked to my father in almost a decade."

Her father would never be parent of the year, but she couldn't imagine him not being a part of her and Max's life.

"Besides," Nathan added, "they're not 'kid' people. Jordan and I were raised by the nanny."

"I think if my mom had lived, my parents would still be together," she said. "I remember them being really happy together."

Her father had loved her mother so much, in fact, that he never got over losing her.

"I don't think mine were ever happy," Nathan said.

"So why get married?"

"My mom was looking for a rich husband and my dad was old money. I was born seven months after the wedding."

"You think she got pregnant on purpose."

"According to my grandmother she did. As a kid you overhear things."

She didn't even know how to respond to that. What a horrible way for Nathan to have to grow up, knowing he was conceived as a marriage trap.

Ana would make it a point to assure Max that even though his parents didn't stay together, he was wanted and loved dearly from the minute he was conceived. Which was exactly what Nathan's mother should have done, whether it was true or not.

Then she had a thought, one that actually turned her stomach. "This is why you thought you wouldn't be a good parent, isn't it?"

"I haven't had the best role models."

He sure hadn't. And why was she was just hearing about this now? Talk about being self-absorbed. Why hadn't she asked about his family when they were dating? Why hadn't she tried to get to know him better?

She thought she loved Nathan, but the truth was, she hardly knew anything about him. Had she been so self-centered, so busy having "fun" that she hadn't even thought to ask? Or was she just too busy talking about herself?

No wonder Nathan had dumped her. If she were Nathan, *she* would have dumped her!

"I'm a terrible person," she said.

He looked genuinely taken aback. "What are you talking about?"

"Why didn't I ever ask you about your family before? Why didn't I know any of this?"

He laughed. "Ana, it's not a big deal. Honestly."

"Yes, it is," she said, swallowing back the lump that was filling her throat. "I feel awful. I remember talking about me all the time. You know practically everything about me. My life is a freaking open book! And here you had all this…baggage, and I was totally clueless. We could have talked about it."

"Maybe I didn't want to talk about it."

"Well of course you didn't. You're a *guy*. It was my responsibility to drag it out of you by force. I never even asked. I didn't even try to get to know you better. I was a lousy girlfriend."

"You were not a lousy girlfriend."

"Technically I wasn't even your girlfriend." She got up from the couch and grabbed their empty cocoa cups. "I was just some woman you had sex with who talked about herself constantly."

She carried the cups to the kitchen and set them in the sink.

Nathan followed her. "You didn't talk about yourself *that* much. And besides," he added, "it was really *great* sex."

# Seven

Ana swiveled to face Nathan, not sure if he was joking or serious, if she should laugh or punch him. And whatever his intention, it hurt.

"That's really all it was to you?" she asked. "Just great sex?"

Only after the words were out did she realize how small and vulnerable she sounded. *Way to go, Ana. Why not just blurt out how much you loved him, and that he broke your heart? Why not throw it all out on the line so you can look like an even bigger fool?*

"What difference does it make?" he asked, his eyes dark. "You were only using me to defy your father."

Ouch. She should have known that remark would come back to bite her.

"And for the record," he said, stepping closer, trapping her against the edge of the counter, "it was not just about the sex. I cared about you."

Yeah, right. "Dumping me was certainly an interesting way to show it."

"I ended it *because* of how I felt for you."

*What?* "That makes *no* sense. If you care about someone, you don't break up with them. You don't treat them like they're the best thing in your life one day, then tell them it's over the next!"

"I know it doesn't make sense to you, but I did what I had to do. What was best for *you*."

For *her*? Was he joking? "How in the hell do you know what's best for me?"

"There are things about me, things you wouldn't understand."

Just when she thought this couldn't get much worse, he had to lay the *it's not you it's me* speech on her. As if she hadn't heard that one a dozen times before. Well, if it wasn't her fault, why did she keep getting dumped? Why was she always the one with the broken heart?

"This is stupid. We covered all of this eighteen months ago. It's done."

She shoved past him but he grabbed her arm.

"It's obviously not done."

"It is for me," she lied, and tried to tug her arm free.

"You weren't the only one hurt, you know."

She made an indignant noise. "I'm sure you were devastated."

His eyes flashed with anger. "Don't do that. You'll never know how hard it was leaving you. How many times I almost picked up the phone and called you." He leaned closer, so his lips were just inches away. "How tough it is now, seeing you, *wanting* you so damned much and knowing I can't have you."

Her heart skipped a beat. He wasn't just telling her what she wanted to hear. He meant every word he'd said.

He still wanted her. And despite everything else that had happened between them, as much as she'd tried to fight it, to be smart about this, she wanted him, too. But she didn't tell him that. Instead she did something even worse. Something monumentally more stupid.

She pushed up on her toes and kissed him.

For one tense and terrifying instant she wasn't sure how he would react, if she was making a huge mistake. But Nathan's arms went around her, his hands tangling through her hair, and his tongue swept across her own in that lulling, bone-melting way of his.

Her knees went soft and her pulse skipped and everything in her screamed *yes!*

He should be telling her that this would only complicate things, and the important thing right now was to keep it civilized, for Max's sake. He should be, but he wasn't.

He broke the kiss and pulled back to look at her, cradling her face in his hands, searching her eyes.

Her heart sank. "Having second thoughts already?"

He smiled and shook his head. "No. Just savoring the moment."

Because it would be their last. She knew it, and she could see it in his eyes. They would get this one night together, then things would have to go back to the way they were. They would have to go back to just being Max's parents. There was no other way. Not for him, anyway. It sucked, and it hurt—boy, did it hurt—but not enough to make her tell him no. She wanted this, probably more than she'd ever wanted anything.

"You're sure this is what you want?" he said, always the gentleman, always worried about her feelings, and her heart, even when he was breaking it. But this one was worth a little pain.

She stepped away from him, grabbed a quilt from the

back of the couch and spread it out on the rug in front of the fire. Nathan watched, his eyes dark, as she stripped down to her bra and panties then laid down on the blanket. He had this look, as though he wanted to devour her, and every part of her hummed in anticipation. Her skin heated and her pulse jumped.

He tugged his polo shirt up over his head, then shoved his jeans off and kicked them aside. He was perfect. Lean and strong and beautiful. The glow of the fire licked and danced across his skin as he got down and stretched out beside her. He propped himself up on one elbow, gazing at her.

"My body is a little different than the last time you saw it," she said.

He touched her stomach, stroking it with the backs of his fingers, and the skin quivered under his touch. "Does that bother you?" he asked.

She shrugged. "It's just a fact."

"Well," he said, leaning over and pressing a kiss to the crest of her breast, just above the lace edge of her bra, "I think you're even sexier than you were before."

As long as he kept touching her, she didn't care how she looked. He eased the cup of her bra aside, exposing her breast to the cool air, and her nipple pulled into a tight point. He teased it lightly with his tongue, then took it in his mouth and sucked. Ana moaned softly and closed her eyes. Nathan reached around to unfasten her bra, working the clasp with a quick flick of his fingers. The low growl of satisfaction as he pulled it off said he either didn't notice that her breasts weren't quite as firm as they had been before, or he simply didn't care.

For a while he seemed content to just touch and kiss and explore her, and oh, could the man do amazing things with his mouth. The problem was, he was only doing them above the waist. And though God knows she loved kissing him, and putting her hands on him was like pure heaven, she was crawling out of her skin, she was so hot for him. But every time she tried to move things along, he would cut her off at the pass.

She enjoyed foreplay as much as the next woman, but even she had limits. But hadn't that always been his M.O.? For him, foreplay wasn't a means to an end. It was an art form. And sex had always been not only satisfying, but fun.

"You know you're driving me crazy," she said.

His grin said that he knew exactly what he was doing. "There's no rush, right?"

"I wouldn't exactly call this *rushing,* Nathan."

"Because I know the second I touch you, you're going to come." As if to prove his point, he slid his hand down her stomach, dipping his fingers an inch or so under the waist of her panties. She bit her lip to keep from moaning, digging her nails into his shoulders, but his smug smile said she wasn't fooling him.

"Well what do you expect after *three hours* of foreplay?" she said.

He laughed. "It hasn't been three hours."

It sure felt like it. He didn't seem to understand that most men pretty much grew bored with the foreplay after five minutes. Nathan, on the other hand, seemed to be going for some sort of world record.

"I'd just like to make this last," he said.

"Did I mention that it's been *eighteen* months? Honestly, I think I've waited long enough."

His eyes locked on hers, and he slid his hand inside her panties again. The second his fingers dipped into her slippery heat she was out on the ledge and ready to fall over. She just needed one little push....

"Not yet," Nathan whispered, pulling his hand away. She groaned in protest. He sat up and tugged her panties off, and she nearly sobbed, she was so ready. Pushing her thighs apart, he knelt between them. He wrapped his hands around her ankles and slowly slid them upward, dipping in to caress the backs of her knees, then higher still, easing her thighs wider. With the pads of his thumbs he grazed the crease where her thigh met her body, then he dipped inward...

She was so close...falling over...

He pressed her legs apart, lowered his head...she felt his warm breath...the wet heat of his tongue...

Her body locked in a pleasure so intense, so beautiful and perfect that a sob bubbled up from her throat. Only when she saw Nathan gazing down at her, brow furrowed with worry, did she realize that tears were leaking from her eyes.

"Are you okay?" he asked. "Did I hurt you?"

She shook her head. "No, it was *perfect*."

"Then what's wrong?"

She sniffled and wiped at her eyes. "Nothing. I think it was just really intense. Maybe because it's been so long. Like a huge emotional release, or something."

He didn't look as though he believed her. "Maybe we should stop."

He was going to back out now? *Seriously?* "I don't *want* to stop. I'm fine."

He sat back on his heels. "You don't look fine."

She pushed herself up, leveled her eyes on him, so he would know she was serious. "Let's put it this way. If you don't make love to me right now, I'll have to hurt you."

Nathan would have had to be a total moron not to realize that Ana was feeling emotional and vulnerable. She was crying, for God's sake. They'd had some pretty intense sex in the past and she'd never burst into tears. And maybe it meant he was a heartless bastard, but he was having a tough time telling her no. Or maybe it was just really hard to think straight with Ana sliding her hand inside his boxers.

"I want you, Nathan," Ana whispered, rising up on her knees beside him, and when she kissed him, she tasted salty, like tears. Despite that, he didn't try to stop her when she pushed him back onto the blanket. Maybe it was wrong, but for the first time in a long time, he didn't feel like he had to be the good guy. The responsible, respectable, never-let-your-emotions-get-away-from-you guy. Being with Ana made him want to *feel*.

It always had.

Which gave this the potential not only to become very complicated, but dangerous, too. Because lately, the self-imposed numbness just wasn't cutting it. And when Ana grasped his erection, slowly stroking him, he sure as hell didn't feel numb. Words could not adequately describe how damned fantastic it felt.

"So, what's it going to be?" she said, looking anything but vulnerable. "Sex, or potential physical trauma?"

Concise and to the point. He'd always liked that about her. When it came to feeling things, Ana had never been one to hold back. She hadn't been afraid to put herself out there. He wouldn't deny that at times it had scared the hell out of him. But at least with her he always knew where he stood. She didn't manipulate or play games. And only because she seemed to know exactly what she wanted now would he let this happen.

He reached over and tugged his wallet from the back pocket of his jeans, fishing out a condom. She snatched it away from him and tore it open.

"You in a hurry?" he asked.

"What part of 'I haven't had sex in eighteen months' didn't you get?"

She might have been surprised to learn that since her, there had been only one other woman for him. And that was over a year ago. A rebound relationship that had been brief and, quite frankly, not very exciting. Of course, compared to Ana, not many women were. That used to be the kind of woman he preferred. Someone who wouldn't excite him or challenge him. But being with Ana had changed him. She'd more or less ruined him for other women. In and out of the bedroom.

"That doesn't mean we can't take our time," he said.

She threw a leg over his thighs and straddled him, and he knew that there was no use in arguing. He could see things hadn't changed. He had a short window of time in which she let him have control—which was nowhere *near* three hours—and then she angled for the dominant position. He knew that when she reached that point, there was no reasoning with her.

She pulled the condom from the wrapper and he braced himself because he knew exactly what was coming next. She'd done it dozens of times before.

With a saucy smile she said, "Goes on better damp," then she leaned down and took him in her mouth. He groaned and fisted the blanket as she used her tongue to wet him from tip to base.

If she kept that up, this would be over in ten seconds.

She sat back on her heels, wearing a smile that said she knew exactly what she was doing to him, and it was payback time. She rolled the condom on like a pro, then centered herself over him, flush with anticipation. Her body was a little rounder than before, her breasts fuller and her hips softer, and he didn't think he'd ever seen anything so beautiful.

"Ready?" she asked.

As if he had a choice.

She braced her hands on his chest and sank down slowly, inch by excruciating inch. He hissed out a breath as her hot, slippery walls closed in around him. Though he would have considered the opposite to be true, he could swear she was even tighter than she'd been before having Max. Maintaining even a shred of control was going to be close to impossible. Ironic, considering the way he'd just been teasing her.

"Oh, Nathan," she moaned, eyes closed, slowly riding him. "You wouldn't believe how amazing this feels."

He wanted to tell her that actually yes, he would, but he was barely hanging on. If he so much as uttered a sound he was going to lose it. And he'd be damned if he was going to let himself climax first. That just wasn't the way he did things. He needed to take the upper hand before he completely lost control.

Nathan flipped Ana over. She let out a gasp of surprise as her back hit the floor. She opened her mouth to protest, but as he plunged himself deep inside of her, a moan of pleasure emerged instead. Arching into his thrust, her legs wrapped around his waist, nails digging into his shoulder. He barely had a chance to establish a rhythm before her body started to quake, clamping around him like a vise, and he couldn't have held back if his life depended on it. In that instant time ground to a screeching halt and there was nothing but pleasure.

When time started moving again, he looked down at Ana lying beneath him, eyes closed, breathing hard, her hair fanned like crimson flames against the blanket. The woman was pure sex.

"You okay?" he asked.

Her eyes slowly opened, filled not with tears this time, but a satisfaction he was pretty damn sure she could see mirrored back in his own gaze. She nodded and said breathlessly, "I know we probably shouldn't have done that, and it's going to complicate the hell out of things, but…damn…it was *so* worth it."

Sex with Nathan had always been out-of-this-world fantastic. But tonight he shot her clear to a different *galaxy*.

She wasn't sure if it was so good because it had been so long, or because it was the first time after having Max. Or if Nathan was just really, really good at making her crazy. Whatever the reason, it was a shame that they could never do it again.

Nathan must have been thinking the same thing. He rolled onto his back, sighed slow and deep, and said, "I guess we should have the talk now."

She threw an arm over her eyes and groaned. "Do we have to? Can't we just enjoy the afterglow for a while?" She looked over at him. "In fact, could we just not talk at all?"

He rolled onto his side and propped himself up on his elbow. She wondered if he had the slightest clue how sexy he looked like that. How difficult it would be to keep her hands to herself now. "You want to wait till later?"

"No, I mean *never*. I have no expectations of this being anything but one time, and I'm assuming you don't either. So, it happened, it's over, end of story. Let's not ruin it by having a conversation."

His this-is-too-good-to-be-real look made her smile. "You're sure about this?"

"It is what it is. Analyzing it to death isn't going to change anything. In fact, it would probably just make things even more complicated. At this point my only concern is Max."

"If that's how you feel."

She really did, for the most part anyway. Did she want more? Of course. Sentiments of love would be nice, and she certainly wouldn't balk at a marriage proposal. Hell, at this point she'd be happy with a semipermanent, exclusive sexual relationship. But she knew that wasn't smart, because ultimately it was going to end, and she refused to put herself in a position to get her heart stomped on again.

There was someone else out there for her. He probably wouldn't be as wonderful as Nathan, or as good in bed. And she would probably never love him the way she loved Nathan, but loving someone too much wasn't such a great thing, either.

"It is," she told him. "I mean, it was probably just something we needed to get out of our systems. You know?"

"Well then, there's a problem."

She frowned. "What problem?"

He lowered his eyes and she followed his gaze down to his crotch.

Oh boy. He clearly hadn't gotten it out of his system yet.

Okay. This was not a big deal. They were already lying here naked, so she couldn't really see the harm in doing it one more time. Or heck, two more times if that's what it took. And since Nathan used to have the libido of an eighteen-year-old, and that probably hadn't changed, it was a distinct possibility.

But after tonight, it was definitely over.

# Eight

Nathan sat in his office the next morning, feeling more relaxed and all around happier than he had in a very long time. Eighteen months, to be exact.

Only problem was, that happiness never lasted.

His life would be going really well, and he would start to think that things were different, that her love had changed him, then something would happen to flare his temper and he would realize that nothing had changed. Wasn't it better to get out while it was still good? Because the last thing he wanted to do was hurt Ana. This situation, their relationship, was supposed to be about Max and what was best for him, yet lately it seemed to be more about Ana and Nathan. Letting this go any further would be a mistake. So, the next time she tried to put the moves on him—and knowing Ana, there would probably be a next time—he would nip it in the bud. He would be the rational one.

Whether she wanted to believe it or not, he knew what was best for her.

His secretary buzzed him. "Mr. Blair needs to see you in his office."

He shoved himself up from his chair and headed down the hall to Adam's office.

"They're waiting for you," Adam's secretary said, gesturing him through the open office door.

*They?* Had he forgotten a meeting? His mind hadn't exactly been in the game the last few days, but that was what his secretary was for, and she hadn't said anything.

Adam sat behind his desk, and Nathan was surprised to see Emilio standing by the window. If it was a scheduled meeting, Jordan wasn't there yet.

"Shut the door." Adam said.

"What about Jordan?"

"I sent him to the refinery."

There was only one reason why Jordan would be excluded from a meeting. There had been some sort of news about the explosion.

He shut the door and took a seat across from Adam's desk. "So I take it there's been a development."

Adam and Emilio exchanged a look, and Emilio said, "Something like that."

He wasn't sure he appreciated the fact that Adam would discuss it with Emilio before him. Until the CEO position was filled, they were supposed to be on a level playing ground.

Nathan sat straighter in the chair, looking from one to the other. "Whatever it is, I see you've already discussed it without me."

"We have a few questions for you," Adam said, looking so solemn that Nathan had to wonder if he'd done something wrong. They couldn't possibly know about Max and Ana.

"So ask," Nathan said.

"I know you and Jordan aren't very close," Emilio said. "But do you know anything about his personal finances?"

"We don't exactly share stock tips. Why?"

"Are you aware of any reason he would have to deposit or withdraw any large sums of cash?"

They were looking into Jordan's personal finances? Had they been checking Nathan out, too? Despite all the animosity he had toward Jordan, that ages-old instinct to defend his brother worked its way to the surface. "Are you accusing my brother of something?"

"A week before the accident someone deposited two hundred thousand dollars into Jordan's account, and a few days later he wired thirty thousand dollars out."

"To whom?"

"I'm afraid we don't have access to that information," Emilio said.

"But what you're saying is, you think he's responsible for the sabotage?"

"You can't deny it looks suspicious."

He looked from Adam to Emilio. "You think that someone paid him, and he paid someone else to tamper with the equipment?"

"That's one possibility," Adam said.

"Why?"

"Jordan is ambitious," Emilio said. "It happened before everyone learned the CEO position was opening up. Maybe he felt he'd hit a ceiling."

"His commitment to this company and his dedication to the men at the refinery has been exemplary," Nathan reminded them. In fact, it was truly remarkable, despite the social and economic differences, how deeply the workers at the refinery respected and trusted Jordan. Not only was he the man in charge, but when he was among the workers, he was one of them.

"Maybe someone made him an offer he couldn't refuse," Emilio said. "But expected something in return first."

"Ambitious or not, I can't see him putting anyone's life in danger to further his career."

"Maybe no one was meant to get hurt, but something went wrong," Adam suggested. "You have to admit, he was the one hit hardest by this. Maybe he feels guilty."

"If he got a better offer, why is he still here?"

"To avoid suspicion? Or maybe now that the CEO position is opening up, he has a reason to stay."

"Or maybe," Emilio offered, "since there were injuries, it killed the deal."

"Look, you know that my brother and I don't have the best relationship, but I'm having a hard time wrapping my head around this." Or maybe he just didn't want to believe that his own brother could be responsible, that he could be that self-serving. Maybe he didn't like that what they were suggesting had credibility.

"Believe me, we don't like it either," Adam said. "But we can't ignore the possibility. If he were involved somehow, and it came out later that we had proof and did nothing about it—"

"You could confront him," Nathan said.

Emilio laughed. "This is Jordan we're talking about. If he's guilty, do you honestly think he'll admit it?"

Good point. Jordan would just as soon slice off a limb than admit he'd made a mistake.

"His secretary will be starting her maternity leave in a few weeks and the investigation firm has suggested we place an undercover operative directly into Jordan's office," Adam said. "He'll just think she's a temp."

"If he finds out, he's going to be *pissed*."

"So we have to make sure he doesn't find out," Adam said. "And we have until then to find another way. Maybe you could try talking to him. Maybe he'll let something slip."

"Honestly, I'm the last person he would confide in. We don't talk. Ever. If nothing else, that would only raise his suspicions."

"If not for Jordan, this company wouldn't be where it is today," Adam said. "If he's innocent, I don't want to risk losing him."

"We took a chance trusting you with this," Emilio said. "I have brothers, so I know it's a lot to ask. But we can only do this if you're behind it one hundred percent."

He knew they were right, and he hated that underneath the need to defend his brother, there was a nagging suspicion that maybe it was true. Either way, they needed to know.

"I'm in," he said.

He knew he was doing the right thing. Still, it felt like a betrayal. But with Jordan's career on the line, maybe this was the best thing he could do for his brother.

Although it got him wondering, as he headed back to his office, if they were investigating Jordan, did that mean he was under investigation as well? But why would he be? He could count on one hand how many times he had actually been in the refinery, and the men who worked there were strangers to him. But if his relationship to Ana and Max were to get out, it could not only hurt his chances at the CEO position but cast doubt over him as well.

He was leaning toward the idea of making Max a permanent part of his life, but at this point it would undoubtedly complicate things. Ana hadn't been pushing him to make any decisions, but he knew it was only a matter of time before she would expect an answer from him. They couldn't go on living in limbo this way. Especially after what happened last night. Which, the more he thought about it, the more he realized what a mistake it probably was. It was clouding his judgement. Making him forget that there were other issues to think about, like whether or not he even deserved to be someone's parent. What if he was destined to repeat his own parents' mistakes? What if he turned out to be like his father, harsh and judgmental? Or, even worse, like his mother? Too absorbed in his own life to care that he had a vulnerable and confused kid desperate for his attention. And if he did lose the CEO position over this, or even his job, would he end up resentful and bitter?

If he could hold Ana off just another few months, until he'd had time to really consider what he was doing, at least until the CEO decision was made…

He'd left his cell phone on his desk, and when he got back to his office there were two missed calls. One from a number he didn't recognize, and one from Ana. Neither left a message. Maybe Ana had decided that they needed to have that talk after all. He was half-tempted to wait and call her back later, until he considered the possibility that her call may have had something to do with their son. What if he was sick or injured? His pulse skipped at the thought.

He dialed her number and she answered on the second ring. In the background he could hear Max babbling happily, and the sudden gush of relief he experienced nearly knocked him back in his chair. In barely over a week, the little runt had managed to weasel his way into Nathan's heart.

The question was, did he deserve Max's love?

"You called?" he asked Ana.

"Yeah. Sorry to bother you while you're working, but

I had something I wanted to ask you. Have you got a minute?"

"Sure."

"I sort of need a favor, but I want to say right up front that you are under absolutely no obligation to do this. I can ask Jenny. I just thought maybe you would want to do it instead."

"Do what?"

"Babysit Max Saturday night. I was invited for a girls' night out with Beth and some of our friends."

"Babysit as in just him and me?"

"Yeah. I thought you might like to get some quality time together. I wouldn't be leaving till seven-thirty, and he goes to bed at eight-thirty, so he'll be asleep most of the time."

The fact that she trusted him to be alone with Max rendered him speechless for several seconds.

"If you don't want to—"

"It's not that I don't want to. I just…I'm a little surprised that you would ask me, considering my vast lack of experience with kids."

"Well, Max adores you, and you know his bedtime routine. Besides, he's pretty easygoing. I can't imagine that he'll give you any trouble. And if you do decide to be a permanent part of his life, you can't keep coming over here and just visiting him forever. You'll have to get used to being alone with him. Sometimes overnight."

The idea both intrigued and made him nervous as hell. He would have to baby-proof his apartment, buy toys and baby furniture. With two extra bedrooms he definitely had the space. These just weren't things he'd taken into consideration before.

"But like I said, if you're not comfortable watching him,

it's okay. I don't want you to think that I'm trying to push you into something you're not ready for."

"No, I'd like to do it," he said, and realized, for all his doubts, he really did.

"Great! Can you be over at my place around seven-fifteen? That will give me time to show you where everything is before Beth picks me up."

"I can do that."

"I don't know what you're doing tonight, but Max and I were going to decorate the tree around seven."

With a dinner meeting scheduled for six-thirty with his team, there was no way he was getting out of work before eight tonight. So he might see him for ten minutes before he went to bed. Meaning he would be going over there to see *her*, not Max, which he didn't think was a good idea after last night.

"I just can't swing it tonight, but maybe I can stop by around lunchtime tomorrow."

"Sure. That would be great." She paused, then asked, "By the way, did you get anything in the mail from Beth and Leo yet?"

"I don't know." He'd brought a pile of mail with him to work this morning but hadn't had time to go through it yet. "Hold on, let me look."

He grabbed the pile and rifled through it until he saw the greeting-card-sized envelope with Beth and Leo's return address. He tore it open, but it wasn't a card. It was an invitation to their annual New Years Eve party. Nathan went every year, except last year, and only because he figured he would run into Ana there. He'd known she was expecting, and the idea of seeing her, pregnant with another man's baby...hell, for all he knew she would bring the father with her. Had he known it was his kid, he might have felt differently.

"I take it you got an invitation too?" Nathan said.

"Yeah. I wondered if you were planning to go. I wanted to, but with us both there...well, it might be a little weird having to pretend we don't like each other."

"We can't stop socializing just because we'll run into each other. That's not fair to either of us."

"I guess not. So you're going to go?"

If only to prove that this thing between them didn't have to be a big deal. "Yeah, I'm going."

"Then I am too," she said.

They talked for a few more minutes about Max, and though Ana never once mentioned what had happened last night, it hung between them unspoken. He could hardly believe he was thinking this, but maybe not talking about it hadn't been such a hot idea after all. Not if it was going to make things awkward. He would probably feel worse if he had been the one to make the first move. Not that he couldn't have told her no. But that would have left her feeling dejected and hurt.

In other words, he slept with her to spare her feelings? How philanthropic of him. Why couldn't he just be honest with himself and admit that he slept with Ana because he wanted to? He *still* wanted to. It would take a hell of a lot more than one night to get her out of his system. Maybe a lifetime of nights. And if she came on to him again, good idea or not, he wouldn't be pushing her away.

He would just have to hope that she didn't.

Only after he'd hung up with Ana, and checked his schedule for his next meeting, did Nathan realize the mistake he'd just made. He was supposed to go to Adam and Katy's holiday get-together Saturday evening. That was what he got for not checking his schedule before committing himself. He'd been so enticed by the idea of spending some real quality time with his son, he hadn't even considered he might have another obligation.

Damn it. Emilio and his fiancée would be there, and he knew his brother would never miss an opportunity to score a few brownie points. Leaving him the odd man out. He could call Ana back and tell her he couldn't make it, but something told him that wouldn't go over really well.

He knew going into this that being a parent would require sacrifice. Besides, Adam had assured him it was okay if he didn't come, that he knew it was last-minute.

Nathan just hoped he meant it. He'd come too far, was too close to getting everything he wanted to throw it all away.

Everything was going to be fine.

Ana sat on the couch, one eye on Max in his exersaucer and one on the clock. Nathan was due there any minute to babysit. And though she was maybe a tiny bit nervous about leaving him and Max alone for the first time, she was crazy nervous about Nathan being here. Their lunch date Thursday—using the word *date* in the loosest of senses—had fallen through, so she hadn't actually seen him since they slept together Tuesday night. They had talked on the phone a couple of times, but that wasn't the same as seeing someone face-to-face.

So much for her brilliant theory about sleeping with Nathan to get him out of her system. All that did was make her want him more, make her fall just a little more in love with him. But what was the point of being in love with someone who didn't love her back?

Easy. There wasn't one.

What had she expected? That sleeping with her was going to make Nathan suddenly realize that he loved her and couldn't live without her? Clearly that wasn't going to happen. She didn't doubt that he cared about her, and desired her. Just not enough to want to spend the rest of his life with her. She was fun in the short term, just not marriage material.

Wasn't that the story of her life?

He may have been *her* one true love, but obviously she wasn't his. And even if he were willing to settle for a life with her and Max, she wanted more than that. She had no illusions about who she was and what she needed from a relationship to be happy. With all her insecurities, she needed someone who adored her. Someone who put his love for her above all else.

Nathan would never be that man. Not for her, and probably not for anyone else. He was too independent, too focused on his own life to devote himself completely to someone else.

The only exception to that rule seemed to be Max.

The bell sounded and she shot up off the couch like a spring. *Jeez, Ana, relax.* She forced herself to walk slowly to the door, glancing at her reflection in the foyer mirror. She didn't get out much these days, so she'd really taken her time getting ready. Usually by this point in the evening she was a disheveled mess, but even she had to admit that she looked pretty hot. Who knows, maybe she would meet someone at the bar tonight. She had wanted to devote her life 24/7 to Max when he was an infant, but he was practically a toddler now, and old enough that she could start thinking about dating again.

If she could just get her mind off of Nathan. She only hoped when she saw him, there wasn't any of that morning-after awkwardness. Even though technically it was more than four mornings after.

Heart in her throat, she pulled the door open. Nathan stood on the porch, looking windblown and sexy as hell.

He usually dressed casually when he came to see Max, but this time he was still wearing his suit.

He looked her up and down, taking in her clingy black cashmere sweater, leggings and knee-high, spike-heeled boots. His eyes widened and he said, "Wow, you look great."

She both loved and hated the warm glow of satisfaction that poured through her veins.

"Thanks," she said, stepping back so he could come in out of the cold. Only when he was inside did she realize how tired he looked, as though he'd been up for several days straight.

"Sorry I'm a few minutes late," he said. "A meeting ran long. I didn't even have time to go home and change."

"You look exhausted."

He shrugged out of his overcoat. "It's been a long week. We're about to go into production with a new ad campaign. Everything that could go wrong has. Thankfully we'll be shutting down for the holidays. I need a break."

From across the room Max let out a squeal and jumped excitedly as he spotted Nathan.

"Hey buddy." Nathan crossed the room to greet him, lifting him out of the exersaucer and hugging him. "I missed you."

Ana's heart melted. "He had an extra long nap today so he might stay up a little bit later for you. Just make sure he's in bed by nine. We have to be up early to get ready for breakfast at my father's house."

"You do that often?"

"A couple of times a month. My father is pretty busy most of the time, but he likes to see his grandson."

"And you, I'm sure."

"No, it's pretty much all about Max. My father and I barely say two words to each other. Unless he's lecturing me on how to raise Max, then he has plenty to say. But it's a one-sided conversation."

"Sounds a bit like my mother," Nathan said. "She loves to hear herself talk. Is your dad single? Maybe we should set them up."

"So you could be my stepbrother? It would be fun explaining that one to Max."

Nathan laughed. "Good point." He gestured to the Christmas tree. "It looks nice."

"We decorated it Wednesday night."

"We?"

"Me and Max, although admittedly I did most of the work."

This wasn't so bad. They were both being incredibly polite, but that beat having nothing to say at all.

Ana glanced at the clock. "Beth is going to be here soon. Why don't I show you where everything is, so I don't have to make her wait." Although the idea of staying home with Nathan and Max was far more seductive right now. But as Beth had implored on the phone the other day, Ana needed to get out and have fun. And she would. She would force herself.

Nathan had already been through the bedtime routine several times, but she showed him where the clean diapers and wipes were, and the pajamas in case Max dirtied the ones he was wearing.

"I left instructions in the kitchen on how to make a bottle, but you've seen me do it before," she told Nathan. "You have my cell number, so don't hesitate to call if you need anything."

"I'm sure I can manage," he said. "Although lately I've developed a healthy respect for parents with young children. People don't realize what a daunting responsibility it is. And you're doing ninety-nine percent of the work."

"It's twice as hard for single moms," she said as they walked back into the living room. "I'm fortunate that I have the financial means to raise my son however I choose. There are so many women who struggle on a daily basis, working two or three jobs to keep up. I've seriously been considering starting a local foundation for single mothers."

"To help financially?"

"Financially, emotionally, whatever they need. We could offer job-training programs and legal help to get support from the deadbeat dads who refuse to own up to their responsibility."

"It sounds like quite an undertaking."

"Which is why I've only *talked* about starting it. For now at least, Max comes first."

"I think you should do it," he said.

It was definitely part of her long-term plans. And she couldn't deny that the idea of being responsible for something so big and important was a bit intimidating. She didn't even know for sure if it would be well received. Especially from someone like her. Despite having changed her ways, the press still liked to perpetuate the "party girl" persona. What if no one took her seriously?

She wouldn't know until she tried.

Outside, Beth laid on the horn.

"That's my ride," she said. She pulled on her coat and grabbed her purse from the foyer table. She considered giving Max a kiss goodbye, but with Nathan holding him it might be a little weird. She blew him a kiss instead and said, "Bye, baby, I love you."

"Have fun," Nathan said.

"You too." She forced herself to walk out the door and down to Beth's car.

"So," Beth said a she climbed in. "First time leaving Nathan and Max alone?"

Ana fastened her seat belt. "Yep."

"Are you nervous?"

"A little, maybe. But I'm sure they'll have fun."

"How about you?" Beth asked with a mischievous smile. "Are you ready for some fun?"

Not just ready, she was long past due.

# Nine

Despite the music and the dancing, and the delicious margaritas, not to mention the men who had asked her to dance, Ana just couldn't seem to relax. All she could think about was Nathan and Max, and how she would much rather be at home with them than in this flashy, overrated meat market. But the flack she would get from Beth if she caught a cab home early wasn't worth the trouble.

What had happened to the carefree party girl? The one who would crawl out of her skin at the thought of a night at home? The one who had always been in motion, always in high gear and looking forward to the next adventure. Had motherhood really changed her so much? Or had it been Nathan? Back when they had first begun dating, she suddenly became not so opposed to the idea of settling down.

"So I guess tonight wasn't such a hot idea," Beth said on the way home.

Was she really that transparent? Beth sounded so disappointed, Ana was overwhelmed with guilt. "I'm sorry. I guess I just miss Max."

"We've been out lots of times since you had Max and missing him never stopped you from having a good time." She glanced over at Ana. "When a drop-dead gorgeous man asks you to dance and you barely give him a passing glance, I'm guessing it has more to do with Max's babysitter."

"I slept with Nathan." She hadn't even meant to tell her. She just sort of blurted it out.

Beth winced. "Okay. I guess I saw this coming."

"It's not going to happen again."

Beth shot her a look. "Of course it isn't."

"I mean it. We both agreed that it was just something we needed to get out of our systems, and now it's over."

"That is the dumbest thing I've ever heard. Get him out of your system? With *sex*? You *love* the guy. Sleeping with him is just going to make you want him more."

"Unfortunately I didn't figure that out until *after* I slept with him. It wouldn't be half as humiliating if I hadn't been the one doing the seducing. Why do I keep doing this to myself?"

Beth reached over and squeezed her hand. "I'm sorry, sweetie. Guys are scum."

"He's actually not. That's the really awful part. He's a great guy. A good man. He's just not the man for me."

Beth pulled up in front of her condo. "But you definitely aren't going to sleep with him again. Right?"

"Definitely not." Especially if that meant making the first move again. She had degraded herself enough.

"You want me to come in with you and stay until he leaves? Just in case?"

"It's after midnight. You should get home." She grabbed

her purse from the floor where it had dropped. "Besides, I think I learned my lesson."

Beth kissed her cheek. "Love you. I'll talk to you tomorrow."

Ana got out of the car, waving as Beth drove away, then she made her way, a bit unsteadily, to the front door. What a lightweight she'd turned out to be. In her party days she could single-handedly drain an entire pitcher of drinks and still ace a sobriety test. Tonight she'd had three margaritas and she could barely walk a straight line.

She unlocked the door and stepped inside, surprised that all the lights were off. So was the television. From the glow of the fire she could make out Nathan's form lying on the couch. He had looked beat when he got there. He must have fallen asleep.

She wobbled on her spike heels, so she tugged off her boots and crossed the room to wake him. But as she got closer she realized it wasn't just Nathan there. Max lay curled up on his chest, head tucked under Nathan's chin, sound asleep. One of Nathan's arms was flung over his head, and the other was wrapped protectively around his son. Sudden tears welled in her eyes, and a lump the size of the entire state of Texas plugged up her throat.

It was, hands down, the sweetest thing she had ever seen in her life.

She sat on the edge of the couch and stroked her son's soft little cheek. He was out cold, and so was Nathan. She rubbed Nathan's arm to wake him.

His eyes fluttered open and he gazed drowsily up at her. "Hey, what time is it?"

"A little after midnight. I take it Max couldn't sleep."

Nathan rubbed Max's back. "He woke up around ten," he said softly. "I think he was upset that you weren't here.

He wouldn't go back to sleep, so I brought him out here with me. I guess we both fell asleep."

"I hope he wasn't too much trouble."

"Not at all. Did you have a good time?"

"Yeah, it was great," she lied. "It's always nice spending an evening with the girls."

"I guess I should get him into bed."

Ana rose from the couch. "You want me to take him?"

"I've got it." He pushed himself gently up from the couch, cradling Max against his chest.

Ana followed them into Max's bedroom and watched as he laid Max in bed and covered him. Max was so dead to the world he didn't even stir. She tucked the blankets around him and smoothed his hair back from his forehead. "Good night, sweetheart. Pleasant dreams."

They stepped out of his room and she shut the door, then they walked to the living room. "Thanks for watching him."

"It was no problem at all."

"So, everything went okay? Besides him waking up, that is."

"Yeah. We had fun." He looked at his watch. "I should get home. You have an early morning."

She wanted to invite him to stay. Offer him a drink, maybe throw herself in his arms and beg him to make love to her.

All the more reason to let him leave.

"I really do need to get to bed," she said, and to herself added, *alone*.

They walked to the foyer. "Maybe I could come by tomorrow afternoon to see Max," Nathan said. "We could get dinner."

Seeing him two days in a row was a bad idea, but she

heard herself say, "Sure. We should be back from my dad's place around one."

"I'll call you then." He pulled on his coat, turned, and with his hand on the doorknob, he just stopped.

She considered saying something snarky, like *the door isn't going to open itself*, but only to hide the fact that her heart was suddenly beating out of her chest. She wasn't even sure why. She just…had a feeling. A feeling that something big was about to happen.

He let his hand fall from the knob and he turned to her. "I don't want to leave."

Her heart rose up and lodged in her throat. *Tell him he has to. Tell him you have to get to sleep. Don't tempt fate.*

"I was going to make myself a cup of tea," she told him instead. "Would you like one?"

"I'd love one."


Nathan stood in the kitchen, watching as Ana put the kettle on to boil, got two mugs down from the cupboard and dropped a tea bag in each one. The truth was, he hated tea. But if choking down a cup meant spending a little while longer with her, it was a sacrifice he was willing to make.

He knew she had to be up early, and if she had told him to leave he would have without question. He had half-expected her to come on to him again. She'd had opportunity. And when she hadn't, he'd felt almost… slighted. He knew they were supposed to be keeping their relationship platonic, for Max's sake, but what if that wasn't enough for him? What if he wanted more?

Which was exactly why he shouldn't be here. It wasn't fair to Ana to lead her on this way. The fact that she looked so damned sexy wasn't helping matters. There wasn't a single thing about her that he didn't find arousing and irresistible. He wanted to believe that she'd dressed that way for him, and not some random stranger she had been hoping she might meet. After all, that was how he had met her. They happened to be at the same bar and Beth had introduced them.

That was assuming she had been at a bar tonight. She hadn't actually said where she was going, just that it was a ladies' night out. Considering the way she'd been dressed, that seemed the logical conclusion. But this was a woman who had worn spike-heeled boots to a six-year-old's birthday party. For all he knew she'd been at a Tupperware party tonight.

"So, what did you and Beth do tonight?" he asked, keeping his voice casually conversational.

"We went with a couple of friends to a new hot spot downtown."

Aka a bar. "How was it?"

She shrugged. "A typical meat market. But the DJ was decent and the drinks weren't watered down."

"But you had a good time?"

"It was…fun."

*How fun?* he wanted to ask, even though it really wasn't any of his business. But what if she had met someone else? Could that be the reason she was giving him the cold shoulder? If that was the case, it sure hadn't taken her long to move on, had it?

The kettle started to boil, so she poured water into the cups. "What do you take in your tea?"

"Sugar." Or for all he knew she could have been seeing someone else this entire time. The fact that she hadn't slept with the guy didn't mean she wasn't planning on it. Maybe she was just taking it slow because of Max.

Or maybe he was letting his imagination get away from

him. He'd seen no hint of any man in her life—no one besides Max, that is.

"So, you go out to bars often?" he asked.

She set his cup, as well as the sugar bowl and a spoon, on the counter for him. "Not lately, but I'm thinking it's about time I get back into the game."

"Which game is that?"

"Dating."

Was she telling him this to piss him off, or make him jealous? Or was she really that clueless to the feelings he had for her? Was she taking this *friendship* thing a step too far? Confiding things he really didn't want to hear?

"You think going to bars is a good place to meet men?" he asked. If she heard the snip in his tone, she chose to ignore it.

She shrugged and said, "I suppose not. I met you at a place like that, and look where it got me."

She sure knew how to hit below the belt. *Way* below the belt.

"Not that I would go back and change things even if I could," she added. "Max is the best thing that ever happened to me."

"It's just me you wish you could remove from the equation," he said.

"That's not what I meant. My point is, men don't go to bars looking for long-lasting monogamous relationships. All I have to do is mention I have a son and they practically run screaming in the opposite direction." She palmed her cup. "Then of course there are the men who would pretend to be Max's best buddy if it meant getting their hands on my trust fund. For a woman in my position, it's hard to know who to trust."

"Maybe until Max gets a little older, it would be better if you just concentrated on taking care of him."

She laughed, but it came out cold and bitter. "That's really easy for you to say."

"How do you figure? Why would you assume it's any easier for me?"

Clearly he'd hit a nerve. She glared up at him. "You can do whatever you want, when you want, and be with whomever you please. With a baby to care for 24/7, I don't have that luxury."

He took a step closer. "For the record, there's only one woman I want to *be with*. But *she* thinks it would be too complicated."

Her eyes widened slightly and she turned toward the window, gazing out into the darkness. "Please don't say things like that."

He stepped up behind her, could feel her shoulders tense as he laid his hands on them. "Why not?"

"Because you know I can't."

And he couldn't stand the idea of her being with anyone but him. He slid his hands down her arms, then back up again. "You don't want me anymore?"

He knew she did, and maybe it was selfish of him, but he wanted to hear her say it. And maybe…maybe this time things could be different. He couldn't even recall the last time he'd let his temper get the best of him. Maybe he'd really changed.

"I do want you," she said softly. "Too much. But I know you'll just hurt me again."

"So, you're finally willing to admit that I actually did hurt you. That's a start."

"I think you should leave."

"I don't want to." He eased her hair aside, pressed his lips to the side of her neck. She moaned softly and leaned back, her body molding against his.

"I can't sleep with you, Nathan."

He eased her sweater aside and kissed her shoulder. He could feel her melting, giving in. "Who said anything about sleeping?"

"Please don't do this," she said, but he could tell she was losing her will to fight him.

"What if things could be different this time? What if *I'm* different?"

She went very still in his arms, and he knew he'd gotten her attention. "What are you saying, Nathan?"

He turned her so that she was facing him. "I want to be with you, Ana. With you and Max."

She looked confused, and terrified. And hopeful. "You're not just saying that to get me into bed, are you?"

"Does that really sound like something I would do?"

She shook her head. "No. But what about work? Your career."

Good question. "We would have to keep our relationship secret for a while. At least until I'm offered the CEO position. Once I'm under contract, they'll have a tough time getting rid of me. Besides, it won't take them long to realize that when it comes to work, my loyalty is to them."

"How long?"

"Adam is resigning in early spring at the latest. He plans to be gone before their baby is born. I'm assuming the new CEO will be announced at least a month prior."

"So, we're talking another three or four months of sneaking around?"

"Worst case, yes. But it could be sooner." He touched her cheek, smoothed back the fiery strands resting there. "After that, I don't care who knows."

She still looked wary, so he pulled out the big guns. "I think we owe it to Max to at least give it a try, Ana. Don't you?"

Whatever fight she'd had left in her, whatever doubts

she still harbored, dissolved in front of his eyes. "I guess if we're doing it for Max…," she said, sliding her arms up around his neck. "As long as you promise not to hurt me again."

"I promise," he said. As he kissed her, lifted her off her feet and carried her to her bedroom, it was a promise he intended on keeping.

# Ten

Ana woke the next morning to the shrill of her cell phone ringing on the bedside table. That was her father's ring tone. She pried her eyes open to check the time on the digital clock—9:05 a.m.

Oh hell. She was supposed to be at his house five minutes ago for breakfast. She had completely forgotten to set her alarm.

She grabbed her phone and flipped it open. "Hey, Dad."

"Where are you?" he snapped. "Did you forget that we had plans this morning?"

"I'm sorry. I forgot to set my alarm and I overslept."

"In other words, you were out clubbing last night, and you couldn't be bothered to drag yourself out of bed at a decent hour so I could see my grandson."

He made it sound as if she'd slept half the day away. It was 9:00 freaking a.m. To this day he refused to even entertain the possibility that she wasn't the irresponsible party girl she'd been before she had Max. And how did he know that she'd gone out last night? She'd tried to keep a low profile, and she hadn't seen anyone who looked like the media following her. Or was he just assuming that because it was the weekend, she would be out?

Defending herself was a waste of time. He wouldn't believe her anyway. "If I get up now and get ready, we can be there in an hour."

"Don't bother. It's clear where your priorities lie. And here I was beginning to believe that you'd finally grown up. Thank God your mother isn't here to see this."

She didn't bother to point out that if her mother were still alive, her life would have been completely different. *Both* their lives.

Instead, she was going to apologize again, and do a little groveling—for Max's sake—but he hung up on her before she got the chance.

Talk about needing to grow up. She mumbled a derogatory term she wished she had the guts to say to his face, then dropped the phone back on the bedside table.

"I take it your dad is pissed off."

Ana nearly jumped out of her skin at the rumble of Nathan's voice beside her. She had just assumed she was alone.

She rolled to face him. He lay on his back, eyes still closed, bare-chested and beautiful. Excitement, and joy, and *hope* bubbled up from somewhere deep inside of her. In all the time they had been seeing each other, he had never once spent the night. Even if they stayed up making love until 4:00 a.m., he always went home. So this could only mean one thing. He actually meant what he'd said last night. He wanted to make this work.

Until that very instant she hadn't been one hundred percent sure. It wouldn't be the first time a man lied to her to get what he wanted. Even though, as far as she knew, Nathan had never lied to her about anything. And though he hadn't told her he loved her, or said anything even remotely resembling a marriage proposal, maybe it was just a matter of time now.

"He was pissed enough to hang up on me," she told him. "And he accuses *me* of needing to grow up. If I did something like that to him, he would freeze me out for months. Maybe even years."

"So let him."

"The only reason I try to keep things civilized is for Max. And maybe I feel a little sorry for my dad. It's pathetic, really, the way he shuts people out. He's been that way ever since my mom died."

Nathan opened his eyes and looked over at her. "That's no excuse."

No, but he was still her father. Although now, with Nathan planning to claim Max as his son, they didn't need her father to be the man in Max's life. Maybe it would be best if she cut all ties, at least for a while. Maybe it would be the wake-up call he needed to see that it was no longer acceptable to treat her this way. "You're right. It isn't. Maybe it's time he learns that."

But not yet. Not until after the holidays. It just seemed cruel to deny him his grandson's first Christmas.

Nathan lifted his arm to make room for her, and she curled up against his side, laid her head on his warm chest, feeling the *thump-thump* of his heart against her cheek. He wrapped his arm around her and kissed the top of her head. "Since you're not going to your father's, why don't you and Max and I go out for breakfast."

"Do you really think that's a good idea? What if someone sees us together?"

"There's a diner I go to by the university. Odds are pretty slim we'll run into someone we know there."

"Okay. That sounds like fun."

"When does Max usually wake up?"

"He should be up anytime now."

Under the covers she felt the warmth of his hand settle on her hip, then slip down to stroke her right cheek. "Do you think we might have time for a quick shower?"

She slid her hand under the covers and down his stomach. He groaned as she wrapped it around his erection and squeezed. "I think it can't hurt to try."

Though he should have put a few hours in at the office yesterday, Nathan ended up spending the entire day and the whole evening with Ana and Max. First they went to breakfast—where no one seemed to recognize them or care who they might be—then they did some last-minute shopping for Max. Because the temperature was mild, they took Max to the park for a while, pushing him on the baby swings and walking him in the stroller down the nature trails. They picked up Thai food on the way back to her place and had dinner, and though he could tell Ana wanted him to spend the night again, he had to be into work early the next morning.

He left after Max went to bed, and when he walked into his apartment, it felt even less like home than usual. If things with Ana and Max worked out the way he was hoping—and he was hoping they would—they would have to think about getting a place together. Preferably a house with a huge yard for Max to play in, in a family-friendly neighborhood with parks. In the current market, he was sure they could get a great deal. But he didn't want to get ahead of himself. He couldn't make a move until he had the CEO position in place.

He spent the rest of his evening online, on the F.A.O. Schwartz website, buying more gifts than Max would probably ever have time to play with, and paying exorbitant shipping prices to guarantee his purchases would be delivered by Christmas Eve. He had already committed himself to dinner with his mother and Jordan Christmas night, but he planned to be at Ana's Christmas Eve after the office party, and Christmas morning when Max opened his presents. It was hard to believe that it was only six days away. And he had a slight problem. He had no idea what to get Ana. She wasn't really into fine jewelry, and besides, that just seemed so…impersonal. What did a man get a woman who had the means to buy herself anything she could ever need or desire?

He wanted to get her something he knew she would really appreciate, something she would never think to get herself. He was in his office Monday morning combing the internet for ideas, waiting for inspiration to strike, when his mother called.

"I've been invited to take a holiday cruise with a friend, so I won't be available to spend Christmas with you and your brother," she told him, without having the decency to sound even the least bit regretful. He was sure wherever she was going would be warm and exotic, and her "friend" was probably significantly older and very rich.

"Well, have a good time," he said, wondering if she heard the relief in his voice.

She didn't suggest they try to reschedule, or even bother to apologize. She just wished him a happy holiday then hung up. His mom, the ice queen. But if nothing else, her call gave him one hell of a gift idea.

He did a quick internet search, finding exactly what he wanted on the first hit. It was perfect!

He considered contacting a travel agent for the finer

details, but with Ana's name on one of the tickets, he decided it was best he did this himself over the internet. He made the arrangements, printed off his confirmation email and cleared the history on his browser five minutes before he was due to meet several members of his team downstairs in the lobby coffee shop.

The meeting lasted through lunch, and just as they were gathering their things to head back upstairs his secretary called. "Your brother is here wondering when you'll be back to your office," she said. "Should he wait or come back later?"

"I'm on my way up now," he said, punching the button for the elevator.

"I'll tell him to wait."

He rode up to the top floor, feeling pretty damned proud of himself for choosing what he considered the ideal gift for Ana. Something she would never expect in a million years. He was out of the elevator and halfway down the hall to his office when he realized that he'd left the confirmation email on his desk. It didn't have passenger names on it, just the itinerary, but that alone would be suspicious. Maybe he would get lucky and Jordan wouldn't look at anything on his desk, though he knew the possibility was slim.

He nodded at his secretary as he passed and stepped into his office to find Jordan standing by the window, looking out. He turned when he heard Nathan walk in.

"What's up?" Nathan asked, walking to his desk. The email was right where he'd left it, on the blotter next to his laptop. He dropped the folder he was carrying on top of it and sat down.

"I suppose she called you," Jordan said.

"I guess there is a Santa, and he gave me exactly what I wanted this year."

"Did she tell you who her new 'friend' is?"

"Nope, and I didn't ask."

"He's a baron. She met him on her last trip to Europe. He's twenty years older than her. Old money."

"There's a shocker."

"I don't suppose you've talked to Dad."

He shot his brother a look. Hell no he hadn't, and for the life of him, he had no idea why Jordan still did.

"He's getting married again."

"How many times does that make?"

"Five. She's a twenty-eight-year-old flight attendant. He met her when he was on a business trip to New York. She's relocating here from Seattle to move in with him."

"I give it six months."

"I know you don't want to believe this, but he's mellowed a lot since we were kids. He asks about you every time we talk. I know he'd like to hear from you."

"That's not going to happen."

"Jesus, Nathan, sometimes I think you're even more stubborn than he is." He started to walk out, then stopped and turned back. "By the way, I just have to ask, what's a single guy doing buying a trip for three on a Disney cruise?"

Inwardly Nathan cursed, but on the outside he didn't even flinch. "Not that it's any of your business, but I didn't book the trip for me. I did it for a friend. He was worried his wife would find out and he wanted it to be a surprise for Christmas."

He couldn't tell if Jordan believed him or not, and maybe it wasn't the best excuse, but it was the best he could do on such short notice.

After several seconds Jordan shrugged and said, "I'd better get back to work."

*Phew.* Tragedy avoided. He hoped.

A few minutes after Jordan left Ana called him on his cell.

"Do you think you can make it over before Max goes to bed tonight?"

"I'll definitely try." Although, having spent most of the morning on the internet, he hadn't gotten nearly as much accomplished as he'd hoped. Which was why, while most of his team were off Christmas Day through New Year's, he would be putting in a few hours in the office.

"Let me know when you think you can get here. I can keep Max up a little late if I have to."

"I will. And by the way, I got your Christmas present today."

He could hear the smile in her voice. "What a coincidence, because I got yours too."

"What are the odds we got each other the same thing?"

She laughed. "Slim to none, and if you did get me what I got you, I'm afraid I would have to seriously rethink our relationship."

"In that case, you don't have to worry. And I should also mention that I picked out a few things for Max, too. They should be delivered on Christmas Eve."

"I almost forgot to ask, what time do you think you'll be finished at your mother's Christmas Day? I was thinking we could meet back at my place afterward."

"I'm not seeing my mother on Christmas."

"Why not? I thought you and your brother were having dinner with her."

"Change of plans. She decided to go on a cruise with a 'friend' instead."

"Seriously?"

"She met him in Europe last month. He's a baron."

"Are you telling me that she ditched her sons for some guy she *barely* knows? That's terrible!"

"That's my mother."

"So, what are your plans?"

"I haven't actually made any yet. Jordan didn't ask what I was doing, so I'm assuming he's got something else planned. I'll probably just hang around my apartment until you get back from your dad's place. When do you typically leave?"

"As early as humanly possible. It's usually just the two of us and it's very…awkward. Although, this being Max's first Christmas, he'll probably expect us to stay longer. I'm still not even sure when we're having dinner. I tried calling him twice today. Once on his cell, then again at his office. His secretary said he was in a meeting, but that usually just means he doesn't want to talk to me. He's probably still pissed about yesterday morning. I think he's convinced that I was out all night partying. There was a blurb in the society pages Sunday morning about me being out clubbing, and someone snapped a photo of me coming out of the bar. The paparazzi is getting really sneaky. I didn't even see them this time."

"And being the devoted father that he is, he of course believes the *press* over his own daughter," Nathan said.

"The ramifications of my rebellious phase. The gift that just keeps on giving."

"He seriously doesn't see that you're not that woman anymore? That you're mature and responsible, and an incredible mother."

"If he's noticed, he's never acknowledged it."

"How is he going to feel when he finds out about us?"

"Truthfully, I don't care anymore. I'm getting tired of the game. If it weren't for Max, I would probably spend Christmas Day at home with you. Preferably next to the fire in my flannel pajamas."

"We'll plan that for next year," Nathan said, realizing

that he was anticipating that there would be a next year for them. And a next, and a next.

"I guess this year we'll just have to settle for Christmas dinner apart. I left my dad a message, but I haven't heard back yet. I'll let you know as soon as I do."

Adam stuck his head in Nathan's office. "Sorry to interrupt. Have you got a second?"

For the boss, always. He gestured Adam inside, noting that he shut the door behind him. "Miss Maxwell, can I call you back?"

He knew Ana would understand that was code for *Someone who can't know who I'm really talking to just walked in.* "Sure. I'll talk to you later," she said.

He shut his cell phone and asked Adam, "What's up?"

"I just wondered if you'd had a chance to talk to your brother."

"About?"

Adam looked a little taken aback. "The suspicious financial discoveries."

Could he make himself look like more of an idiot?

"Sorry, but no, I haven't." Lately he'd been too wrapped up in his own life to give it much consideration. "Like I said the other day, Jordan and I just don't talk. I was supposed to have dinner with him Christmas Day, and I thought I might be able to get something out of him then, but the plans fell through. But even that was a long shot. If I start prying into his personal finances, he's going to get suspicious."

"I understand. I wanted to ask anyway, just in case. It looks as though we'll have to go through with replacing his secretary with an agency operative. He'll be told that she was sent by our temp company."

"I really think that's going to be the best way to get the

information we need. Although for the record I still believe he's innocent."

"I hope that's the case." Adam turned to leave, then stopped with his hand on the doorknob and turned back to Nathan. "Is everything okay with you?"

"Of course. Why do you ask?"

"Lately you've seemed a bit…distracted. That, and you've been taking more time off than usual."

"Do you have an issue with my performance?"

"No, not at all. And in case you're worried, it isn't something that will have a negative impact when it comes to your bid for the CEO position. I consider you a friend, and I was concerned."

Though Adam didn't come right out and say it, Nathan could tell that he wanted some sort of explanation. Considering the circumstances, and put in his position, Nathan would feel the same way. "The truth is, I've been seeing someone," he told Adam. "It's still pretty casual at this point, but it has definite possibilities."

"I'd like to meet her. Will you be bringing her to Emilio's wedding?"

"Unfortunately I don't think she's available." Available or not, there was no way he could bring her. Which wasn't fair to either of them, but it was the way it had to be.

"First I got married, now Emilio is tying the knot." Adam grinned. "Maybe you'll be next."

"Yeah, let's not get ahead of ourselves."

"Settling down, having a family, it's not such a bad thing, Nathan," he said, as he walked out.

He wished he could tell Adam that he already had the "having a family" part nailed down. He wanted to be able to brag about his son, show photos around the office and to his friends.

Just a few more months, then and he and Ana would be home free.

# Eleven

This was ridiculous.

It was four on Christmas Eve night, and Ana still hadn't heard one word from her father about Christmas dinner the next day. She had called him half a dozen times this week, leaving messages, asking him to please call her back. She had even resorted to apologizing yet again about Sunday morning, and telling him how wrong she was.

That was yesterday, and he still hadn't acknowledged her.

She looked at the clock, knowing Nathan would be there any minute, then she glanced at the phone, wondering if she had time to give him one more quick call.

Why? Why should she call him again? She already apologized and practically begged his forgiveness. Maybe he thought that making her spend Christmas alone was the ultimate punishment. Although she couldn't see him passing on an opportunity to shower Max with gifts.

Knowing him, he would wait until the absolute last second to pick up the phone and expect her to be at his beck and call. It was astounding that a man responsible for running a multi-billion-dollar corporation could exhibit such childish behavior. Well, she was sick of playing his games, and it was time he realized that. Nathan didn't have any plans for dinner tomorrow and she would much rather spend the evening with him anyhow.

If her father didn't call by the time Nathan got here and she made other plans, he would miss Max's first Christmas.

Feeling only slightly guilty, she dropped her phone on the kitchen counter. She turned toward the open bottle of wine breathing on the table to pour herself a glass, but the doorbell chimed.

Four o'clock, right on time. Maybe she should think about giving Nathan a key, so he could let himself in from now on. She dashed for the door, and pulled it open.

"Merry Christmas!" Nathan said, grinning as he stepped inside.

Before he could even get his coat off, she threw her arms around his neck and kissed him. It wasn't until she backed away that she noticed the ornately wrapped box in his hand. It was around the size of a shirt box, only thinner.

He handed it to her. "Do you have room for this under the tree?"

"Barely," she said, nodding to the Christmas tree and the dozens of wrapped packages that had arrived earlier that day. "Did you buy out the entire store?"

"Close to it, I think." He shrugged out of his coat and followed her into the living room, where she set the gift under the tree near the front. "Where's Max?"

"Taking his afternoon nap. He should be up any minute. Would you like a glass of wine?"

"I'd love one."

"So, you're technically on holiday break?" she asked as they walked to the kitchen.

"I may stop into the office for a few hours between now and New Year's to catch up on a few things, but my entire team is gone. My only other plans are to spend as much time as possible with you and Max."

She poured two glasses of wine and handed him one. "I have a proposition for you."

"Okay," he said.

"How would you like to have Christmas dinner with your son this year?"

His brow wrinkled. "What's wrong? Did something happen with your dad?"

"No. In fact, absolutely *nothing* has happened. He still hasn't called me back. For all I know he isn't going to. I'm tired of these silly little mind games. So I decided I would just make other plans."

"And if he calls at the last minute, expecting you to come?"

"I'll regretfully decline."

"You're sure about this?"

"Absolutely." She rose up on her toes to kiss him. "There's no one else in the world Max and I would rather spend the holiday with."

He grinned and wrapped an arm around her waist, pulled her against him. "In that case, I accept."

"We'll have to run to the grocery store after dinner. For a turkey and all the trimmings. I've never actually made one, but I'm sure I can find a recipe on the internet."

"If we can even find a turkey. I imagine the stores will be pretty cleaned out by now."

"Then we may have to settle for grilled cheese and tomato soup. That's about all I have right now. My dad always sends me home with so many leftovers, I didn't stop at the market this week."

Nathan grinned down at her, smoothed her hair back and kissed her softly. "As long as I'm with you and Max, I really don't care what we eat."

That just might be the sweetest thing anyone had ever said to her. Even though it was last-minute, and she hadn't had time to plan, she wanted to make their first Christmas together a special one.

From the baby monitor she heard Max beginning to wake up. "You want to get him while I look for recipes?"

He gave her one more sweet, bone-melting kiss, then went to get their son.

Ana spent the next hour online, discovering that not only was there *a* turkey recipe, there were about ten thousand! She chose one for turkey and stuffing that sounded tasty and looked fairly easy to pull off, then she assembled a shopping list of everything she would need, hoping that the stores wouldn't be as cleaned out as Nathan had predicted. When she was finished they packed Max up and went to the diner for dinner, then stopped at the market on the way home. The small, privately owned organic place she usually went to was out of everything. They tried the larger commercially owned organic store a few miles away, but they too were cleaned out of all the holiday fixings.

They packed Max back up into the car and tried the national grocery chain store next. Though it was packed to the gills with last-minute shoppers, they hit pay dirt in the meat department. Not only did they have turkeys, but they were already thawed, which she had learned online often took days. The only problem was the smallest they had was twenty-six pounds.

"We're going to be eating turkey for a month," Nathan said, dropping it in their cart.

Probably, but she didn't care. She probably wouldn't have even cared if they never found a turkey. Spending the evening with him and Max, shopping together as a family, was more than she ever could have hoped for.

They hit the produce department next, and she was relieved to find that they carried organic versions of most of the items she needed. They picked up three different varieties of pies in the bakery department, plus the bread they would need for the stuffing. By the time they got in the checkout line—which had to be twenty carts long—their shopping cart was practically overflowing. They stood in line discussing their plans for the next day, and by the time their things were rung up and bagged, it was way past Max's bedtime. He fell asleep in the car on the way home, and Ana got him into bed while Nathan brought in the groceries and got his overnight bag from the trunk of his car.

He offered to help her put everything away, but she shooed him out of the kitchen and insisted he go watch TV. When he snuck back into the kitchen half an hour later for a beer, he was dressed in flannel pajama bottoms. And nothing else.

Arms folded, she looked him up and down. "Are you trying to lure me out of here?"

He grinned. "Is it working?"

She licked her lips. "If I didn't have about a million things to do…"

He gave her a quick kiss. "Actually, it was too warm with the fire going. But if you're not finished in here soon, I may have to take you against your will."

After he was back to watching TV, Ana put the rest of the groceries away and prepared things for the following morning, thinking how absolutely perfect the evening had been. Almost too perfect, just like the last time.

Everything seemed to be going really well then, too, and out of the blue he'd dumped her. Maybe if she knew for sure why he had done it then, she wouldn't worry now. Or maybe she should stop being paranoid and be thankful for this second chance.

It was past eleven when she shut off the kitchen light and headed out into the living room. The television was still on, but Nathan was lying on the couch asleep. She grabbed the remote from the coffee table and switched it off. Though they should probably get to bed so she could get up early to start the preparations for dinner, she had this sudden, soul-deep need to be close to him.

She undressed and dropped her clothes in a pile on the floor then climbed on the couch, straddling Nathan's thighs. He must have really been out cold because he didn't even budge. She considered gently shaking him awake, but wondered how far she could go, what it would take to wake him in other, more fun ways.

She leaned over, pressed her lips to his hard stomach, trailing kisses down until she reached the waist of his pajamas. She stopped to check his face, but his eyes were still closed. Other parts of him, however, were waking up. She hooked her fingers under his waistband and eased it down, and he didn't even stir. Leaning over him, she first teased the tip of his erection with her tongue, and when that got her no response, she took him in her mouth.

She heard a moan, then felt his hands on her head, his fingers tunneling through her hair. That was more like it, she thought, taking him in even deeper.

She sat back, and Nathan smiled up at her with heavy-lidded eyes. "At first I thought I was dreaming," he said. "It's not often a man wakes up to find a gorgeous naked woman on top of him."

She grinned. "Well then, maybe I should do it more often."

"I could get used to that." He cupped her face, pulled her down for a slow, deep kiss. He stroked her bare shoulders and her back, sliding his hands down to cup her behind, then he tugged her forward, bucking upward, so that his erection rubbed her just right. She dug her nails into his shoulders, moaned against his lips. With one slow, deep thrust he was inside her.

It felt so damned good, but she couldn't shake the feeling that something was missing. Then it hit her. No condom.

Damn it, damn it, damn it.

He was moving inside of her as she slowly rode him, no barriers, nothing to come between them, feeling so close to him, so connected. She didn't want to stop. But intercourse without a condom, even if they stopped and put one on now, was like playing Russian roulette. And she had the proof of that sleeping down the hallway. But her period was due in two days, so the chances that she would conceive were pretty slim.

But that wasn't a decision she had any right to make alone.

She pushed herself up, bracing her hands on Nathan's chest. "We have to stop."

He groaned an objection, thrusting upward. "No we don't."

"We forgot to use a condom."

"I know."

"You *do*?"

He laughed lightly, stroking his hands up her sides, cupping her breasts as he thrust upward once, then twice, making her crazy with need. "Did you honestly think I wouldn't notice?"

"You don't care?"

"I was going suggest we grab one, but I thought I would be polite and satisfy you first."

"I'm pretty sure that's how I conceived Max."

"So are you saying it's too late? The damage is already done?" He said it so casually, as if they were talking about the weather. She figured he would be at least marginally concerned at this point, but he kept up those slow, deep thrusts.

"My period is due soon, so odds are pretty good that I'm not even fertile, but there's always that million-to-one chance."

"Are you opposed to the idea of having another baby?"

"Well, no, but—"

"Then let's not worry about it."

Well, if he wasn't going to worry, if he was comfortable with the consequences...

Nathan tugged her back down to him, kissed away the last of her doubts, his hands, his mouth making her crazy, until she was so close...

He caught her face in his hands and looked in her eyes. "I love you, Ana."

Those four, simple words drove her over the edge, and Nathan was right behind her. After, she tucked her head under his chin, limp and relaxed, and Nathan held her.

It was hard to believe how much had changed in only a few weeks. It felt too good to be true. In a way she almost wished she *would* conceive, then he would have to stay with her.

As quickly as the thought formed, she knew how wrong it was. And dangerous. Not to mention untrue. Besides, why would she even think that she needed a way to trap him? He said he loved her, that he didn't care if she got pregnant again. Everything was perfect.

And if it was so perfect, why this feeling of unease? And if she loved him, why hadn't she said so?

Nathan woke to the aroma of fresh coffee.

It was barely 8:00 a.m., but Ana's side of the bed was empty. He rolled onto his back and rubbed the sleep from his eyes. Last night on the couch had been pretty incredible. He used to believe that she was too passionate to be good for him, that she would make him lose control. What he hadn't understood, but what was becoming clear now, was that she was exactly what he needed. The passion he felt for her was like a vent for all the pent-up negative energy. She kept him centered.

She was the one who would save him, the one he could depend on to keep him in line. She would teach him to be a good father. To Max, and maybe to another baby. Right now, the possibilities seemed endless. And all he knew for sure was that he needed to move forward.

He rolled out of bed wondering if Max was up yet. He couldn't wait to see his face as he opened all of his gifts.

He tugged on his pajama bottoms and a sweatshirt, then went looking for Ana. The Christmas tree lights were on, and holiday music was playing softly in the living room. She was in the kitchen, wearing pink flannel pajamas, an apron tied around her waist, washing dishes by hand. The turkey was already stuffed and resting in a pan on the stove.

When she saw him she smiled. "Merry Christmas."

"Good morning. I smell coffee."

She gestured to the coffeemaker with her elbow. "I just made a fresh pot."

He walked behind her, looping his arms around her waist, and kissed her cheek. "How long have you been up?"

"Since six. I wanted to get the turkey ready to go in the oven before Max woke up."

He watched over her shoulder. "Is there anything I can do to help?"

"You could pour us some coffee while I finish these dishes. I heard Max stirring, so he should be up any minute now."

As if on cue, they heard a screech from the baby monitor.

"On second thought," Ana said, "why don't you get him and I'll pour the coffee?"

When he got to Max's room, he was standing in his crib, clutching the railing. He squealed happily when he saw Nathan.

"Merry Christmas, Max. Are you ready to open presents?" He lifted him out of his crib, quickly changed his diaper—which even he had to admit he was getting pretty good at—and carried him out to the living room. Ana was waiting with their coffee and milk for Max. Nathan sat on the couch, and Max curled up in his lap to drink his bottle.

Just as they got settled Ana's cell phone started to ring. She rolled her eyes and said, "Ugh. It's my dad."

"You don't have to answer it," Nathan said.

"No. I refuse to play that game with him." She snatched it up off the table and flipped it open. "Hello, Dad."

She listened for several seconds, then said, "I've been calling all week. When I didn't hear back I assumed you weren't having dinner this year and I made other plans." Another pause, then she said, "No, I will not change my plans. I have a stuffed turkey waiting to go in the oven."

Nathan could hear her father in full rant clear through the phone.

"I regret that the food will go to waste. If you had called

me back and let me know—" More yelling from his end. "No I am not trying to be difficult. I just can't—" She lifted the phone away from her ear, snapped it shut and shook her head. "He hung up on me. Apparently dinner was at three."

"Are you okay?" he asked.

She shrugged and tossed her phone onto the table. "It's his loss. He needs us more than we need him."

She was right. They were a family now. Her father had become the odd man out. And Nathan couldn't help feeling a twisted sense of satisfaction over that. Professionally, Ana's father was at the top of his game, respected and feared. Personally, he was a miserable excuse for a human being.

"So," Ana said, smiling at Nathan and Max, "Who wants to open presents?"

# Twelve

Ana sat curled up on the couch in front of the fire, sipping coffee and watching Max play with his presents, although he seemed to be having as much fun with the boxes as the actual toys. Nathan sat on the floor by the tree, assembling all of the "some assembly required" items. He had loved the "World's Greatest Dad" beer mug from Max, and the San Antonio Spurs season tickets from her. And she still couldn't believe he had booked them a week on a Disney cruise! Honestly, she had expected something less original, like fine jewelry, for which she'd never really formed an affinity. She inherited all of her mother's jewelry and wore that when the event necessitated it. But a trip, just the three of them, where no one would know or care who they were, sounded like heaven on earth.

Overall, she would have to say this had been a pretty awesome Christmas so far. Despite her father's call. She couldn't even work up the will to be angry about it. She just felt sorry for him. He didn't know her at all anymore. Maybe he never had. And the really sad part was that he didn't even want to try.

Oh well, his loss. Maybe if she held her ground, and refused to let him manipulate her any longer, it would force him to take a good hard look at himself.

Although somehow she doubted it. She'd always just assumed he started acting this way after her mother passed away, but what if he'd always been so self-centered and stubborn? Ana was only six when her mom died. Maybe her memories of them as a happy family were nothing but childish fantasies.

"Finished!" Nathan said, holding up the assembled toy triumphantly.

"And it only took you an hour," she teased.

He got up from the floor and sat beside her on the couch. "I have to admit, I have a new appreciation for all the toy assembly my father did over the years. Although I could have done without the shouting and cussing."

"In our house the butler assembled the toys."

He slipped an arm around her shoulder and pulled her close. "Things will be different for Max."

She leaned her head against his shoulder and smiled. "I know."

For a long time they sat there together, listening to Christmas music, watching Max play. Eventually Ana had to get up and put the turkey in the oven, then she got all the side dishes prepared, and the potatoes peeled and ready to boil. When Max went down for his afternoon nap, Ana and Nathan crawled into bed and made love. Afterward, Nathan fell asleep, so Ana showered, dressed and checked the turkey's progress. It still had another hour to cook, but it was already a deep golden brown and smelled delicious. So far so good.

She'd left her phone on the kitchen counter with the ringer off, and when she checked the display she saw that there was a missed call from her father at 3:05 p.m. Maybe he thought she'd been bluffing, and was probably calling to find out why she wasn't there. She hoped he learned a lesson from this, but knowing him, he would only accuse her of being selfish.

Well, that didn't matter anymore. She couldn't make him see something that he didn't want to see.

Ana straightened up the living room, stacking all of Max's new toys back under the tree until she could decide on a permanent home for them. At four she heard Max begin to stir and was about to go in and get him when the doorbell rang. She wasn't expecting anyone, and most people didn't just stop by on Christmas Day.

She walked to the door and pulled it open, her jaw dropping in surprise when she saw who was standing on her porch. "Dad, what are you doing here?"

"Since you insist on being stubborn, I had no choice but to bring Max's gifts to him."

*She* was stubborn? Was he kidding? "Now isn't a good time."

"Who is it, Ana?" Nathan asked from behind her, holding Max, both still wearing their pajamas, hair mussed from sleep. Her father shouldered his way past her through the door. When he saw Nathan he blinked in surprise.

"Who the hell is this?" he asked, looking from Ana to Nathan, then his eyes narrowed, and she could tell the instant recognition set in. He turned to her, jaw tense, teeth gritted. "Why am I not the least bit surprised?"

"It isn't what you think," she said.

"Is this how you punish me? By consorting with the competition?"

That stung, but she tried not to let it show. Besides, hadn't it started out that way?

He turned to Nathan. "If you'd kindly hand over my grandson, then you can get dressed and get the hell out of my daughter's house."

Nathan didn't even flinch. He met her father's eye, wrapped an arm protectively around Max and said, "There's no way in hell I'm handing my son over to you."

"Max is *this man's* son?" Ana's father growled, and Nathan had the feeling he'd just opened one big fat can of worms, but he hadn't been able to keep his mouth shut. He'd be damned if he was going to let that arrogant bastard boss him around. Nathan's role as Max's father trumped the position of grandfather any day of the week.

"Yes, Nathan is Max's father," she said, with no apology, no regret.

"Ana what in *God's* name were you thinking?"

"This is none of your business, Dad."

"The hell it isn't. Where was he when you were pregnant? For the first nine months of Maxwell's life? Or have you been seeing him all this time? *Lying* to me."

"Nathan didn't even know about Max until a few weeks ago. But he's here now."

"Not if I have anything to do with it." He turned to Nathan. "I understand you're in line for the CEO position at Western Oil. I can only imagine how your connection to my family will go over with the board."

Nathan tensed. He should have seen this one coming. "I suppose I'm about to find out."

"No you won't," Ana said. "Because my father isn't going to tell anyone. Because if he does, he'll never see his grandson again."

Her father scoffed. "Maxwell adores his grandfather. You would never keep him from me."

"If you ruin the career of the man I love, you're damned right I would."

He blinked. "You're not serious."

"You don't think so? *Try me.*"

"In that case, I want a paternity test. I want proof that he's Maxwell's biological father."

Nathan opened his mouth to tell him to go to hell, but Ana spoke first. "*You* want? Because I don't see that's it's any of your business. That's between me and Nathan. Who, for the record, never even asked for one. He trusts me, unlike my own father, who apparently thinks I was slutty enough to be sleeping with multiple partners."

He leveled his eyes on her. "Well, it wouldn't be the first time, would it?"

Ana sucked in a breath, and Nathan's temper shot from simmer to boil in a heartbeat. If it wasn't for the fact that he was holding Max, he might have actually taken a swing. But for his son's sake, he clamped a vise down on his anger. He stepped in front of Ana, saying in a very calm and even tone, "You're talking about the woman that I love. And that is the *last* time you will ever speak to her that way. Understand?"

Maybe her father realized he'd gone too far, because he actually backed down. "You're absolutely right, that was uncalled for. I'm sorry, I didn't mean it."

"I'm going to get Max dressed," Ana said softly, taking him from Nathan, leaving Nathan alone to deal with her father.

That wasn't the sort of thing Ana was just going to forget, and he had the feeling her father realized that. Though Nathan thought he was getting exactly what he deserved, a part of him was sympathetic. He knew what it was like to lose his temper and say or do things he later regretted. The difference was, he'd been man enough to learn how to control it. Maybe this would be the wake-up call her father needed. Maybe he and Ana could begin to repair their fractured relationship.

After an awkward silence, her father said, "I have gifts for Max. Should I bring them in?"

He was actually asking Nathan's permission? Maybe he figured he had better odds with Nathan than with Ana. And unless her father was doing something to hurt Max, Nathan didn't feel it was his place to stand between him and his grandfather.

"Sure, bring them in."

He opened the door and gestured to the man standing on the front walk. He'd been stuck in the cold waiting, his arms filled with packages. His driver, Nathan was assuming, when he saw the Rolls Royce parked at the curb.

It took the man three trips back and forth to bring it all in, while Nathan and Ana's father stood not speaking. This was definitely not the way Nathan had expected to spend his Christmas. Families had a funny way of screwing up plans.

"So," Ana's father said, when his driver had brought in the last of the gifts and gone back to the car. "Do you have plans to marry my daughter?"

He should have expected this. Still, the question caught him a bit off guard. "The thought had occurred to me."

"I supposed it's too much to expect you to ask my permission."

Was he kidding? At this point he would be lucky to get an invitation to the wedding. "I can't see that happening."

"I suppose you'll be expecting a job with my company, and a corner office."

Could the guy be more arrogant? Did he think the

entire world revolved around him? "I already have a job," Nathan said.

His brow furrowed. "I'm not sure I like the idea of my son-in-law working for a competing company."

Nathan didn't give a damn what he liked or didn't like. And he would have a serious problem working for someone like Ana's father, especially if he turned out to be the one responsible for the sabotage. Besides, he hadn't even proposed yet. Nor did he have any plans to in the immediate future.

Ana appeared in the foyer, holding Max. She'd dressed him in his Christmas outfit. "Have you eaten yet?" she asked her father.

"No."

"Would you like to stay for dinner?"

He glanced over at Nathan. "If it's not an imposition."

Did he suddenly see Nathan as the man of the house, or was he just afraid of making the wrong move?

"Why don't you take Max while I finish dinner and Nathan showers," Ana said. He removed his coat and took Max from her, carrying him into the living room. Ana gestured Nathan down the hall, and he followed her into her bedroom. She closed the door and leaned into him, wrapping her arms around his waist, burying her face against his chest.

"You okay?" he asked, rubbing her back.

"After what he said to me, am I crazy for inviting him to stay?"

"If he meant it, maybe, but I don't think he did. I think he probably felt threatened and was lashing out without thinking. Men like him are used to being in control. Take that control away and they say and do stupid things."

"I guess that makes sense." She lifted her head and gazed up at him. "Thanks for defending me."

"You defended me first. Did you really mean what you said?"

"What part?"

He touched her cheek. "When you said that I'm the man you love."

"I did mean it." She rose up on her toes to kiss him, whispered against his lips, "I love you, Nathan."

Those four words made his whole holiday. The ultimate Christmas gift. Women had said it before, but it hadn't meant half as much coming from anyone else. No one knew him, or understood him, the way Ana did. "I love you, Ana."

Her lips curved into a smile. "I better get back into the kitchen before I burn dinner."

"I'll be in to help you in a minute."

She gave him another quick kiss, then left him alone. While he was in the shower he could swear he heard the doorbell, but he couldn't imagine who else could possibly stop by. Maybe it was the driver, or he could have been hearing one of Max's new toys.

He shaved, and dressed in a polo and slacks, then headed out to help Ana. The second he stepped into the living room he saw that there was in fact someone else there and was incredulous when he realized the man sitting on the floor playing with Max was his brother, Jordan.

In that instant this went from one of the best Christmases of his life, to the holiday from hell.

Jordan saw Nathan standing there and rose to his feet. "Hey, big brother. Merry Christmas."

"What the hell are you doing here?" Nathan asked.

"He came by when you were in the shower," Ana said, walking into the living room, wiping her hands on her apron. That part was pretty obvious. Unless Ana had been hiding him in a closet all morning.

Ana's father was sitting on the couch, looking amused by the entire situation.

"Is there something wrong with wanting to spend Christmas with my brother? And my *nephew*?" Jordan asked.

Nathan shot a look Ana's way.

"I didn't say a word," she said. "He already knew."

Nathan looked at Jordan questioningly.

"You've been acting weird for weeks," Jordan said. "Then you give me that lame excuse about the cruise. You insult my intelligence, Nathan."

They needed to have a word. Several, in fact. But he wasn't going to do this in front of Ana and her father. And especially not Max.

"Why don't we step outside," Nathan said.

Jordan scoffed. "It's cold and raining."

"Don't be a sissy," Nathan shot back, realizing, when the false cheer slipped from Jordan's face, that he sounded just like their father. Somehow his family always managed to bring out the worst in him.

Jordan walked to the door and grabbed his coat. Nathan pulled his own coat on and followed him out onto the porch. It was cold and damp and the sky was spitting down icy rain.

"Isn't this cozy," Jordan said, dropping all pretense of holiday cheer. "You spending the holiday with Ana Birch and her daddy. I guess now we know who to blame for the sabotage."

"Jordan, do you really think I could do that?"

"You can't deny this looks pretty damned suspicious."

"Not that it's any of your business, or I feel I need to justify my actions in any way, but her father wasn't supposed to be here. He just showed up, which I'm sure you can understand. Besides, I wasn't even seeing Ana when it happened. I didn't even know I had a son until a few weeks ago. I broke up with her before she knew she was pregnant."

"Did she think it was someone else's?"

He gritted his teeth and glared at Jordan.

Jordan shrugged. "Just a thought."

"She planned to raise the baby alone."

"What if *she's* responsible for the sabotage?"

*"Ana?"* That was the most ridiculous thing Nathan had ever heard. "Not a chance."

"Why not? What if she was bitter and wanted to get back at you for dumping her? Or maybe she did it for her father."

"She wasn't exactly lusting for revenge. If anyone had the right to be pissed, it was me. And as for her father, they aren't exactly on the best of terms."

"He's her meal ticket."

"She lives off a trust left by her mother. She doesn't get a penny from Birch Energy. And even if she did, she doesn't have a malicious bone in her body." Nathan had to wonder, if Jordan really was responsible for the sabotage, would he so vehemently try to blame someone else? Or was that just his way of deflecting suspicion off himself? Had he caught on that he was being investigated?

Nathan had been quick to defend Jordan, but he honestly didn't know anymore.

"How did you find out that it was Ana I was seeing?" Nathan asked.

"I followed you, genius. You're not exactly 007, you know."

Apparently he wasn't, not that he'd expected someone to be tailing him. "How did you know Max is my son?"

"I didn't. Not until I saw him up close. He looks just like you, and the birthmark was a dead giveaway." He blew hot air into his hands, then stuck them into his coat pockets. "Are you going to marry her?"

That was the second time he'd been asked that question today. "I'd say there's a good possibility."

"You know that's going to mean a job offer from old man Birch."

That's the second time that had come up, too. "Why would I want to work for him when I'm CEO of Western?"

Jordan grinned. "You've got to get through me first."

"I plan on it."

Jordan shivered and stamped his feet. "It's cold as hell out here. Can we maybe go back inside now?"

Nathan folded his arms. "Who said you're invited?"

"You would make your baby brother spend Christmas alone?"

"My baby brother who just accused me of sabotage."

Jordan shrugged. "Okay, so maybe I overreacted."

"And how do I know you're not going to run to Adam and the board with this?"

"I'm ambitious, but that would just be too easy. I prefer a fair fight. Besides, I guess I owe you one."

It was the first time Jordan had ever acknowledged what Nathan had done for him. *Who knows,* Nathan thought, *maybe there is hope for us yet.*

The front door opened and Ana stuck her head out. "Sorry to bother you, but everything is ready. I just need someone to carve the turkey."

Jordan shot him a questioning look.

"Do you mind if my brother stays for dinner?" Nathan asked her.

"We've got plenty of food," she said, then added sternly, "But I *do not* want my son's first Christmas to turn into World War Three. As long as everyone plays nice, it's fine with me."

Jordan flashed her a charming, borderline flirtatious smile. "I always play nice."

He did, Nathan thought wryly, *right up until the second I turned my back and the knife came out.* But it was Christmas, the season for forgiveness, and for his son's sake, Nathan would put aside the bitterness and be a family.

# Thirteen

As they sat down to dinner, Ana warned everyone that she wasn't much of a cook, and to eat at their own risk. And maybe it was beginner's luck, or she had hidden talents, because the meal was hands down the best Christmas dinner Nathan had ever had. Even her father, who Nathan had the feeling was not typically liberal with the compliments, raved about the food. Nathan hoped that now he would see how talented and resourceful Ana really was. In many ways she was still the woman he'd met a year and a half ago, only so much more, and he was proud of the person she had become.

Jordan, who in contrast was very liberal with the compliments, whether he meant them or not, seemed genuinely impressed. Nathan was surprised that despite the mixed company, the evening wasn't nearly as awkward as he would have expected. It probably helped that everyone deliberately avoided the subject of the oil business. Even her father seemed to realize that he was on shaky ground. He seemed humbled. Maybe his making that comment, hurtful as it was, was a blessing in disguise.

Ana's father left at seven-thirty, and Jordan hung around playing with Max until it was time for him to go to bed. If nothing else, it looked as though he would be a good uncle.

"He's a great kid," he said, after Ana took Max into his room to get him ready for bed, and Nathan walked Jordan to the door. "What is it with all the kids lately? It must be something in the air. First you, then Adam, now Emilio."

"What about Emilio?"

He pulled on his coat. "That's right—you left the party yesterday before he made his announcement. His fiancée is pregnant. They just found out. I didn't think *anything* could shake that guy. He's like granite, but I think he may have actually been a little misty-eyed. He looks really happy."

"There's definitely something to be said for finding the right woman," Nathan told him. "Maybe you'll be next."

"The problem I find is that there are so *many* right women, I'm not sure which one to choose."

Nathan grinned and shook his head. "It'll happen. Probably when you least expect it. You'll meet someone and you'll just know."

"Was it like that with Ana? Because I recall you saying that you broke it off."

"And it might have been the worst mistake of my life. I'm just lucky that she was willing to give me a second chance."

"You're getting sentimental, which can only mean you've had way too much to drink."

Actually he was stone-cold sober, but he didn't argue.

Jordan slugged his arm. "Go sleep it off. And Merry Christmas."

"Merry Christmas. And drive safe." He watched his brother disappear into the night, then he shut and locked the door and set the alarm.

He found Ana in the kitchen washing dishes by hand. "Is the dishwasher broken?"

"It's already full and running. This is what's left."

He stepped up behind her, slipped his arms around her waist, nibbled her ear. "Are you sure you don't want to leave these for tomorrow?"

"It's tempting, but I really hate waking up to a dirty kitchen." She smiled up at him hopefully. "If we do it together it'll take half the time."

Half the time ended up being an hour. When they were finished, they heated mugs of spiced cider in the microwave then cuddled up on the couch in front of the fire. Ana had barely spoken since everyone left, and Nathan was beginning to wonder if something was wrong.

"Is everything okay?" he asked her. "You've been awfully quiet."

She sighed and rested her head against his chest. "Just tired. It's been a really long day."

"That it has."

"It didn't work out exactly as we planned, but I think it went okay."

"Better than I anticipated, considering the guest list."

"It was really strange opening the door and seeing my dad there. And even stranger when your brother showed up."

"Yeah, that was definitely unexpected."

"He was really good with Max. I wouldn't have pictured him as a kid person."

"As long as it's someone else's, I guess. He doesn't seem to have any desire to settle down and have a family of his own. Of course, neither did I."

"This is probably a terrible thing to have to ask, since he is your brother, but he's not going to say anything to the board at Western Oil about us, is he? I know that you were concerned about him finding out."

"He said he wouldn't. He said he wants a fair fight."

"And you trust him?"

"You don't?"

She shrugged. "Maybe it's because of the things you've told me, or just a gut feeling, but it seems as though he really resents you."

"He has no reason to resent me. I saved his hide more times than I can count. He *owes* me."

She lifted her head and looked up at him. "Saved it from what?"

"Our father. He was a hard-ass, and he liked making his point with a belt, or the back of his hand, or sometimes even his fists."

Her eyes went wide. "Your father *hit* you?"

"I told you before, he was a bully."

"I just figured that you meant he bossed you around. I didn't think he was physically abusive. And you protected Jordan from him?"

"Jordan is younger than me, and up until college he was small for his age. Real quiet and shy. I was tougher, and a lot bigger, so I took the knocks for him."

She was staring at him, mouth open in awe. "You let your father hit you instead?"

He wasn't sure why that came as such a surprise to her. Maybe because she was an only child. "I was the oldest. It was my responsibility to watch out for Jordan."

"It seems like it should have been your father's responsibility to find a more constructive way to discipline his children. Or your mother's responsibility to protect you both. Why didn't she stop him?"

"She probably didn't want to risk losing her meal ticket."

"So she let her husband abuse her children? That's just *wrong*. They put people in jail for that sort of thing. I believe it's called depraved indifference." She wasn't just mildly disturbed, she was furious. Maybe because she was looking at it from the point of view of a parent.

"It's not worth getting this upset, Ana. It was a long time ago."

"It's just not fair," she said, reaching up to touch his cheek. "You should have had a better childhood. It's not right that your parents failed you so badly."

"Maybe, but the world doesn't always work the way it should."

"And look at all you've done with your life, despite it. You're the CBO of a billion-dollar company. That's a huge accomplishment."

"You want to hear something weird? Your dad sort of offered me a job."

She laughed. "Seriously?"

"He said he didn't like the idea of his son-in-law working for a competing company."

"Did you remind him that you're not his son-in-law?"

"Well, not yet. He was talking about the not-so-distant future."

Her brow crinkled. "Are we planning to get married in the not-so-distant future? Because I think I missed the memo."

"Unless you don't want to marry me," he said.

She sat up and set her cup on the coffee table. "I didn't say that. I just didn't know that *you* wanted to. We've never actually talked about it."

Of course they had. "I told you I wanted to make this work, that I wanted to be with you. Eventual marriage seemed like a foregone conclusion."

"A single woman never takes that for granted. And when she does, she tends to get her heart filleted and handed back to her in little pieces."

It took him several seconds to connect the dots, and when he did, he understood why she wouldn't take anything he said for granted. "You're talking about me, right? When we were seeing each other before Max."

She shrugged. "I thought everything was going great, that we had a future. You kept telling me how happy you were. Then pow, out of the blue you dumped me."

"I guess I did, didn't I?" He pulled her into his arms and held her. She snuggled up against him, soft and warm. She was so tough all the time, so direct and resolute, he sometimes forgot that she had a sensitive and vulnerable side. She'd gone through life probably feeling abandoned by her mother then rejected by her father. Then Nathan came along and made her feel wanted, and he let her down, too. He wasn't going to let that happen again. Besides, he needed her as much as she needed him. He needed to show her that he meant what he said. That this time it was different.

"I have an idea that I wanted to run past you," he said.

She tilted her head back and looked up at him. "I'm listening."

"I've been thinking that eventually we're going to need a bigger place. Something single-family, with a big yard for Max. Because of work, I thought it would be best to wait, but it is a buyer's market. It couldn't hurt to start searching now."

She sat up a little straighter, looking as though she wanted to let herself be excited, but she was still wary. "Are you sure? What if we find something right away?"

"Worst case, we could move in and I can keep my apartment as my formal mailing address. Although I doubt anyone would question me buying a house. Emilio, our CFO, owns investment properties all over."

She still looked unsure.

"If you don't want to, we can wait," he said.

"It's not that at all. I want this. I really do. It's just... everything is happening so fast."

"And it seems to me that it's about a year and a half past due."

"I just don't want us to rush into anything. I want *you* to be sure."

"I am sure." It was the most sure he had been about anything in a very long time. Ana grounded him. He would be a fool to let her go again.

She smiled. "Okay then. Let's look for a house."

"I'll call an agent after the first of the year." They would have to work out the logistics of actually viewing the properties, since they couldn't be seen together house hunting, but they would figure something out.

She leaned back against his chest and sighed. "I'm exhausted."

"Why don't you go crawl into bed. I'll get the lights and check on Max."

She yawned and shoved herself up from the couch. "I'll see you in there."

As she shuffled off, yawning and rubbing her eyes, Nathan shut off the lights and unplugged the Christmas tree. On his way to bed he slipped into Max's room. He was asleep on his stomach, and as usual he'd kicked the covers off.

Nathan tucked the blanket up around his shoulders, then he pressed a kiss to his fingers and touched them to Max's cheek. When the three of them were living together, he could do this all the time, since odds were pretty good that he wouldn't be home every night in time to tuck Max into bed. A lot of women would have a problem with their husbands or significant others working such insane hours, but Ana grew up around the oil business, so it was second nature to her. Even back when they were dating the first time she'd never made an issue out of his work schedule.

Nathan closed Max's door behind him and walked to the bedroom, pulling his shirt over his head, wondering if Ana was too tired to make love. He got his answer when he stepped into the room and heard her slow, even breaths from under the covers.

She was out cold.

He put on his pajamas and crawled into bed, curling up behind her. She murmured something incoherent and cuddled against him. And as the digits on the clock neared midnight, he couldn't imagine a better way to end his Christmas than lying in bed, holding the woman he loved.

So why did he have a nagging voice in his head saying that things were so good, so perfect, something was bound to go wrong?

# Fourteen

"Are you sure that you and Nathan are okay?" Beth whispered, taking Ana's empty champagne glass and handing her a fresh one. "You've barely even looked at each other all night."

"That's the point," Ana said, sipping the champagne, knowing that if she was going to make it to midnight she was going to have to pace herself. She and Nathan had already arranged to meet upstairs in the guest bedroom right before the clock struck twelve so they could share a New Year kiss. And maybe share a little more than that. From the minute she poured herself into the crimson party dress, he'd been gunning to get her back out of it again. And though he looked utterly delicious in his tux, she much preferred what he was hiding underneath it.

Since Christmas Eve, Nathan had spent every night at her place. Every day he brought more of his things, and he'd arranged for the service that picked up and delivered his dry cleaning to start coming to her condo instead of his apartment.

If someone had told her a month ago that she and Nathan and Max would be more or less living together now, she would have called them crazy.

Beth handed the empty glass to a passing waiter and asked Ana, "So you two are bitter rivals tonight?"

"No." She glanced over at Nathan, who was standing across the room with a group of elegantly dressed couples. He seemed to sense her watching and glanced her way. Other than the slight tilt of his lips, he did nothing to acknowledge her. "Just indifferent," she told Beth. "Sometimes acting as though you hate someone is even more suspicious than not acknowledging them at all."

"Ma'am?" One of the servers approached Beth. "We're running short on cocktail napkins."

"There's another box in the pantry," Beth told her, and she stared at Beth blankly. Beth sighed and said, "I'll show you."

They walked off in the direction of the kitchen, and Ana crossed the great room to the Christmas tree beside the stone fireplace. It put hers to shame. It was so tall it nearly kissed the peak of the vaulted ceiling. There was another equally grand tree in the foyer at the base of the staircase. Beth always went all out on the holidays, enlisting a professional to decorate the estate inside and out. In fact there were so many white lights adorning the house and the trees and shrubbery throughout the grounds, Ana was sure that it was visible from space.

"That's quite a tree," Nathan said, stepping up beside her, as though he was just making polite conversation with a fellow party guest.

"Yes it is," she agreed.

He leaned in and said softly, "Sort of puts ours to shame."

She smiled and whispered back, "Funny, but I was just thinking the same thing."

"Next year," he said.

"If we want one this big we'll need a great room with a vaulted ceiling."

"Should we put that on the list?"

In preparation for house hunting, they had begun making a list of the features they both wanted in a home. Nathan had even been looking at available properties online and already found several possibilities. Ana just wished she could shake the feeling that things were moving too fast.

Was it that she'd been hurt so many times that she was afraid to trust it, or was it her instincts telling her something was wrong? She just wasn't sure.

"Ana Birch?" someone said from behind her.

She turned to find a short, plump, vaguely familiar woman. She had blond, poofy hair that accentuated her round face, and wore a dress that was just a smidge too clingy for someone her size. "Yes?"

"It's me, Wendy Morris!" she bubbled excitedly. "From St. Mary's School for Girls!"

It took a second, then Ana was hit with the memory of a young, bubbly cheerleader wannabe who was always so desperate to be accepted by the popular girls she made an annoyance of herself. "Oh my gosh, Wendy, how are you? I haven't seen you in ages."

"Well, it's Wendy Morris-Brickman now," she gushed proudly, flashing a ring in Ana's face. She turned and shouted across the room, "Sweetie, come here!"

A man who looked to be about Nathan's age, with thinning hair and round glasses, in a tux that didn't quite accommodate his stocky build, crossed the room. Wendy hooked an arm through his in what looked like a death grip. He couldn't have been more than two inches taller than his wife, and though Ana wouldn't have considered him unattractive, he was very…nondescript. Bordering on mousy.

"This is David Brickman, my husband. David, this is Ana Birch, my good friend from high school."

More like casual acquaintances, but Ana didn't correct her. She accepted David's outstretched hand. It was warm and clammy.

"Nice to meet you," he said, but she realized he wasn't even looking at her. His eyes were on Nathan, who was still standing beside her.

Wendy looked up at Nathan and asked Ana, "And this is your…?"

"Nathan Everette," he said, shaking her hand, then extending his hand to David.

David looked at his hand, then glared up at Nathan, red-faced with anger.

What the heck?

"You have no idea who I am, do you?" David asked.

Nathan blinked, and she could see him wracking his memory.

"We attended Trinity Prep together," David said, with a venom that took Ana aback.

Who was this guy? And why would he be so openly rude?

Nathan must have recognized him, because suddenly all the color drained from his face. "David, of course," he said, but he looked as though he might be sick.

"Let's go, honey," David said, dragging his confused wife in the opposite direction.

"What the hell was that about?" Ana whispered.

"Later," Nathan said, before he walked away, too.

She couldn't exactly go after him, not without rousing suspicions, but she wanted to know what was going on. Maybe Beth would have an idea.

Sipping her champagne, she walked to the kitchen, but Beth wasn't there. In fact, she didn't see her anywhere. Beth was the consummate hostess. She would never just disappear in the middle of her own party.

Ana found Leo in the study showing off his college football trophies.

"Have you seen Beth?" she asked him.

"She's probably upstairs freshening her lipstick," he said.

Ana headed up the stairs to the master suite. The door was closed so she knocked gently.

"I'll be down in a minute!" Beth called.

"It's Ana. Are you okay?" she said.

There was silence, then the door opened. And Beth clearly was not okay. Her eye makeup was smudged and tears streaked her cheeks.

"Beth, what's wrong?"

She pulled Ana into the room and shut the door. "I'm just having a minor meltdown. I'll be okay in a minute."

"Did something happen?"

Beth sat on the edge of the bed. "It's nothing."

"It's obviously not *nothing* or you wouldn't be crying."

"It's Leo," she said with a shrug. "You know how men are."

"What did he do?"

"I went in the pantry to get the napkins and he was in there." At Ana's questioning look she added in a shaky voice, "With a paralegal from his firm."

Oh hell. "I take it they weren't in there getting napkins."

Beth laughed through her tears. "Not unless they were crammed down her bra."

"That rat bastard," Ana said, furious on Beth's behalf. She'd seen him two minutes ago and he hadn't looked the least bit remorseful. She always thought that Leo was the perfect father and husband, and that he and Beth had the ideal marriage. So much for that delusion. "Do you think it was a minor indiscretion, or is he having an affair?"

"There have been a lot of late nights at the office the past month or so, and calls on his cell phone that he has to take in his study. And our sex life has ceased to exist, so I'm guessing she's the new flavor of the month."

"The *month?* Are you saying that he's done this before?"

"Usually he's much more discreet. He's never brought one home. At least, not that I've known about. He always says that he's sorry, and it won't happen again, but it always does. I thought that when we got married he would settle down, that I would be enough."

He was screwing around on her in *college,* too? And she *still* married him? "Beth, why do you let him treat you this way?"

"I love him. Besides, what choice do I have? I don't want to be a divorced single mom. My parents adore Leo. He's from a good family and he has the perfect career. They would be *horrified.*"

Ana loved her aunt and uncle, but they always had been too hung up on appearances. "Screw your parents. You have to do what's right for you."

Beth dabbed at her eyes. "I'm not like you, Ana. I'm not strong. I don't like to be alone."

"You think I'm strong? Beth, I'm the most insecure person on the planet. But I'd rather be alone and miserable than with someone who had so little respect for me that he would cheat. You deserve so much better than that. And think about the message you're sending your daughter."

"There's no way she could know. She's too little."

"She is now, but unless you put a stop to this, eventually she's going to figure it out. Do you want her to think it's okay to let her husband cheat on her? Do you want her to go through what you're going through right now?"

She bit her lip and shook her head. "Are you terribly disappointed in me?"

"Of course not! I love you and I'm always going to be on your side. I just want you to be happy."

"He looked really sorry, and he said he would end it, and it wouldn't happen again. Maybe he means it this time."

And why would he stop when he knew he could get away with it? When the only repercussion of his actions was making his devoted wife miserable.

"Beth, you need to do something. If you don't want to leave him, then tell him you want to go to marriage counseling."

"But my parents—"

"Forget your parents. Do what's best for you and Piper." She took Beth's hand and gave it a squeeze. "I'll stand right by you, and help you in any way that I can."

"I'll think about it," she said, then she dabbed her eyes and squared her shoulders. "I need to fix my face and get back downstairs to my guests. It's going to be a new year soon."

And for Beth, Ana feared it was going to be an unhappy one. No matter what she decided.

Ana left her alone to pull herself together and headed back downstairs, wishing there was something she could do or say to help Beth, to make her see that she didn't have to put up with that kind of treatment. Especially from a man who supposedly loved her.

She nearly ran into Nathan as he climbed the stairs.

"Where did you go?" he whispered, even though there was no one in the immediate vicinity to hear him.

She jerked her chin up toward the second floor. "Bedroom. We need to talk. You would not believe what just happened."

"Actually, I was just leaving."

"*Leaving?* As in going home? But…Jenny has Max all night. We can stay out late."

"I'm not much in the mood for celebrating."

What the hell? How could a night that had started out so well suddenly crash and burn?

"Is it because of David Brickman? Why was he so rude to you?"

"It's a long story."

"One I'd love to hear," she said, grabbing his sleeve and leading him back upstairs to the guest bedroom where they had planned to rendezvous.

When they were inside with the door closed, he asked, "So, what happened with you?"

"Not me. Beth. She caught Leo in the pantry in a compromising position with a woman from work. She said he's been cheating on her for years. Even back in college, before they were married."

"I know."

He mouth fell open. "You do?"

"I lived in the same house with him for two years. He didn't exactly try to hide it."

"Why didn't you ever say anything?"

"What was I supposed to say? Who am I to pass judgment on anyone?"

"So you think that sort of behavior is acceptable?"

He sighed. "Of course not."

"How can you even be friends with someone like that?"

"He didn't cheat on me. What Leo does or doesn't do, and who he does it with, is none of my business."

Ana took a deep breath and blew it out. "You're right. I didn't mean to snap at you. I'm just so *angry* right now. At Leo for hurting Beth, and at Beth for putting up with it."

"I know." He reached for her, pulled her into his arms and just held her. It was exactly what she needed.

She rested her head against the lapel of his jacket, breathed in the scent of his aftershave. The guy sure had a knack for making her feel better. And she knew that he would *never* be unfaithful to her.

"So what's the deal with that David Brickman guy? Why was he so rude to you? Oh, and for the record, I was not 'good friends' with Wendy in school. I barely knew her. And she obviously has pretty lousy taste in husbands."

"Actually, he was completely justified."

*"What?"* She looked up at him. "How? What did you ever do to him?"

"There are things about me, things I haven't told you. Things I would rather forget."

"Like what?"

"You know how there's always that kid in school, the one who preys on the smaller, weaker kids? The kid who's always getting into trouble, getting into fights?"

"Of course. Is that who that guy was?" If so, he was probably the shortest, least threatening bully in history.

"No, that was *me*."

Her mouth dropped open and she actually laughed, the notion was so completely ridiculous. "Nathan, you are the nicest, most patient and caring man I have ever met."

"That wasn't always the case. My dad bullied me, so I went to school and bullied kids who were smaller and weaker than me. The therapist I was seeing said it made me feel empowered."

"You saw a therapist?"

"In high school. It was court mandated as a part of my probation."

*"Probation?"*

"After I put my father in the hospital."

She sucked in a breath. "What happened?"

He sat down on the edge of the bed and she sat beside him. "I had gotten suspended again for fighting, and as usual that meant a beat-down from my father. But I don't know, something inside of me just snapped, and for the first time I fought back. I laid him out in one punch, and as he fell he cracked his head open on the credenza. I was arrested for assault."

"It sounds more like self-defense to me."

"The police didn't think so. Of course, they didn't get the whole story. My mother sided with my father, of course."

That was just sick.

"On the bright side, that was the last time he ever laid a hand on me, so it wasn't a total loss. And the therapy did me a world of good. It helped me learn to deal with my anger. Although to this day it can still be a struggle."

She was having some anger issues of her own right now. Between Beth's husband and Nathan's parents, she was beginning to get the feeling that there was no justice in the world. The worst part was that she had the distinct impression that despite everything he'd overcome and accomplished, Nathan still believed he was damaged somehow.

And she feared there wasn't a damned thing she could do about it.

# Fifteen

Nathan was in the conference room with his team going over the final schedule for the television spot that would begin shooting the next day, when a call came in from Adam.

"I need to speak with you," he told Nathan, and something in his tone said it wasn't going to be great news. Maybe there had been a development in the investigation.

"Can it wait?" he asked. "We're almost finished in here."

"No, it can't."

Okay. "I'll be right in."

He told his team to finish up without him then took the elevator up to the top floor and walked to Adam's office, a knot in his gut. He hoped this didn't have anything to do with Jordan, and that they hadn't discovered more evidence to incriminate him. Seeing Jordan on Christmas Day, watching him play with Max, had given Nathan hope that he and his brother might repair their damaged relationship. Of course, he still wasn't sure what had damaged it in the first place. But things didn't seem as tense now as they used to be.

"Go right on in," Adam's secretary said.

Adam sat behind his desk, his chair turned so he was facing the window. He must have heard Nathan come in because without turning he said, "Close the door." When Nathan did, he said, "Have a seat."

Nathan did as he was asked. He was a little surprised that Emilio wasn't there, too. And why wasn't Adam saying anything? After a minute of silence, Nathan asked, "Am I supposed to guess why I'm here?"

Finally Adam turned to him, face stony. "I've had some disturbing news today."

"From the investigation firm?"

Adam shook his head. "From another source. But it relates to the investigation."

"Is it about Jordan?"

"No, it's about you."

Nathan's pulse skipped. "Me?"

"I've been told that you have ties to Birch Energy. That you have a connection to the owner's daughter and recently had a meeting with Walter Birch himself. Tell me that they're wrong."

Son of a bitch.

It was Jordan. It had to be. This was his idea of a *fair fight*?

Nathan clenched his fists, digging his nails into his palms. If he was going to explode, he couldn't do it here. And he had no choice but to tell Adam everything. "I did not have a *meeting* with Walter Birch. We both spent Christmas Day at his daughter's place."

Adam's brows rose. "Why?"

"I'm in a relationship with Ana Birch," he said. "And we have a son."

Adam looked truly stunned. "Since when?"

"I only recently found out he's mine," Nathan said. "About a month ago. Before that I hadn't actually seen or talked to Ana in a year and a half."

"So you weren't in contact with her at the time of the accident," Adam said.

"No, I wasn't."

Adam looked relieved. "This source didn't outright say that you were the saboteur, but it was heavily insinuated."

Thanks Jordan. So much for brotherly devotion. "Don't think for a second that I don't know who this 'source' is. Besides Walter Birch, my brother is the only other person who knows about my relationship with Ana. He was there on Christmas during this so-called meeting."

"This person seemed genuinely concerned, Nathan."

"He's not. He just wants to win. And apparently he'll do anything to make it happen. Including making false accusations against his own brother." And after Nathan had *defended* him. Well, never again. They were finished. As soon as Nathan was done with Adam, he and his baby brother were going to have a talk. Probably their last.

"How serious is the relationship?" Adam asked.

"We're planning to get married. But that will in no way diminish my loyalty to Western Oil."

"I believe that, but convincing the rest of the board won't be so easy. You can't deny that there is a clear conflict of interest."

"Are you telling me that my job is at stake?"

"As long as I'm president, your job is secure. But if the rest of the board finds out it could take you out of the running for the CEO position. In fact, I can almost guarantee it."

"So what you're saying is, I'm screwed."

"I said *if* the board finds out. I'm not going to tell them, but I also can't stop anyone from leaking the information."

"You don't think the board will see through his attempts to discredit me?"

"In light of the sabotage, I think the board will see it as a legitimate concern. Our first board meeting of the year is next Wednesday. If it comes up, I will do whatever I can to defuse the situation. But I can't promise anything. All I can tell you is that unless there is proof of a direct violation to the terms of your contract, your current position is safe. And as far as I'm concerned, there's no basis whatsoever for termination."

But his chances at the CEO position were basically in the toilet—and even if they weren't now, Jordan wouldn't rest until they were.

Nathan left Adam and walked straight to Jordan's office, his anger mounting every step he took.

"Is my brother in?" he asked Jordan's very pregnant secretary.

"Yes, but he asked not to be disturbed."

*I'll bet he did,* Nathan thought, walking right past her desk, ignoring her protests, and shoving through the door. Jordan was sitting behind his desk, feet up, talking on the phone. Startled, he jumped to his feet when Nathan barged in.

"Can I call you back?" he said to whoever was on the line, and after he hung up said, "Geez, Nathan, you ever hear of knocking?"

Nathan slammed the door. "You sleazy, back-stabbing son of a bitch."

Jordan's brow rose. "Is there a problem?"

"Do not insult my intelligence. Did you honestly think I

wouldn't know it was you who ratted me out? That I'm too stupid to figure it out? This is your idea of a fair fight?"

Jordan shrugged. "The way I look at it, there's nothing unfair about what I did."

"And it doesn't bother you in the least that you just betrayed your own brother?"

He walked casually around his desk, as if he didn't have a care in the world. "This has nothing to do with the fact that we happen to be related. This is business. I'd think you would know the difference."

Nathan crossed to where his brother stood. "You looked me in the eye and lied to me, Jordan. After all the years I watched out for you, and protected you—"

"Who asked you to?" Jordan growled, so fiercely Nathan actually flinched. "I never needed or *wanted* your help."

"You don't give a damn about anyone but yourself, do you?"

"I'm going to beat you, Nathan. And it has nothing to do with experience, or education, or who's stronger. The fact of the matter is, I'm not screwing the daughter of our direct competitor, and you are." He stepped closer, getting in Nathan's face. "Although from what I've read, you're probably not the only one."

Before he even knew he'd swung, Nathan's fist connected solidly with Jordan's jaw, knocking him back several feet. That was how it was with his temper. It came out of nowhere, blindsiding him. And after he'd spent the better part of his childhood protecting his baby brother, never did he imagine being the one doing the hitting.

Jordan dug a handkerchief out of his suit jacket and pressed it to the corner of his bleeding mouth, but he was smiling. "All that therapy, and you still turned out just like him."

Jordan's words sliced through Nathan, cutting to the core. He was right. After all these years, hadn't he learned that using his fists was never the answer?

Suppose someday Ana really pissed him off? Or Max? Would he lose control and hit them, too? He thought being with Ana had changed him, made him a better man, but he had obviously been wrong. He stormed out of Jordan's office and walked blindly to the elevator. What kind of man would he be if he put his own child and that child's mother in danger?

A monster. And that was exactly what he was.

He took the elevator down to the lobby and headed out to the parking lot to his car, so rattled that he barely recalled the trip there as he pulled into Ana's driveway. He used his key to get inside, but she and Max weren't there.

Good, it was better that way.

He went to the bedroom, grabbed a duffel bag out of the closet and started stuffing his clothes inside, marveling at just how many of his things he'd managed to bring over in a week's time.

What the hell had he been thinking?

He was in the bathroom grabbing his toothbrush and razor when Ana appeared in the doorway.

"Hey, what's with the duffel—" She actually jerked back when she saw his face. "Oh my gosh, you're white as a sheet. What happened?"


Ana thought for sure that Nathan was going to tell her someone had died.

"I have to leave," he said.

"Why? Where are you going?"

"Back to my apartment," he said, and at her confused look added, "Permanently."

She felt the color drain from her face and her heart plummeted to her toes. "You're dumping me?"

"Trust me when I say you're better off without me. You both are." He pushed past her and walked back into the bedroom, tossing his things into the duffel bag sitting on the bed.

*No,* this could not be happening. Not again. "Nathan, please, tell me what happened. Did I do something wrong?"

"You didn't do anything." He zipped the bag shut. "Jordan ratted me out."

Damn it. She *knew* it. She knew they couldn't trust him. "So you're leaving me so you can still be CEO?"

"It has nothing to do with work. It's me. I confronted Jordan, words were exchanged, then I hit him."

If her brother had betrayed her that way, she would have hit him, too. "It sounds like he deserved it."

"Violence is never the answer. It's not safe for you to be around me. Not you and especially not Max."

"Nathan, that's ridiculous. It's one thing to get in a fight that's unprovoked, to bully someone, but Jordan betrayed you and you lost your temper. You would never do anything to hurt me and Max."

"Are you sure about that? And is it a chance worth taking?"

"I'm one hundred percent sure."

"Well, I'm not." He grabbed the bag and headed out of the room.

She followed him. "No! You are not going to do this to me again, damn it!"

He pulled the front door open and she hurled herself at it, slamming it shut again.

"We need to talk about this, Nathan."

He gazed down at her, looking tired. Tired and resigned. Just the way he'd looked the last time, and she knew in that instant that he wouldn't be changing his mind. "There's nothing to say."

The ache in her heart was so intense she winced. "You said you wouldn't hurt me."

"I thought I'd changed. I was wrong."

"What about Max? He needs you."

He shook his head. "He's better off without me."

He put his hand on the doorknob, but he wouldn't look at her. She could stand there blocking the door until hell froze over, but he was still going to leave. He was already long gone. Walking out the door was just a formality now.

She moved away from the door and he pulled it open. He had one foot on the porch when she blurted out, "If you leave, this is it. I'm not giving you another chance. Not with me or Max. Walk out that door and you're out of his life forever."

He paused, half in, half out of her life, and a kernel of hope bloomed in her chest. Maybe faced with the reality of losing them permanently would shake some sense into him.

He turned, looked her in the eye, and her heart started to beat wildly.

*Please, please don't do this.*

"I'm sorry, Ana," he said, then he stepped out the door and was gone.

After he left Ana's condo that night, Nathan drove around for hours. He knew he should go home, but his apartment just wasn't home any longer. He finally rented a hotel room and slept there, and that was where he'd been staying for the past week. And as for work, he'd been functioning on autopilot.

He missed Ana and Max. He hadn't even known it was possible to miss someone as much as he missed them.

There was a gaping hole in his heart, in his soul, and the essence of who he was, and the desire to live the life he'd worked so hard building, was slowly leaking out. Before long, there would be nothing left but an empty shell. Without them in his life, he felt, what was the point?

He hadn't talked to his brother since the day of their confrontation, but Wednesday morning Jordan knocked on Nathan's office door. Nathan should have told him to get lost, but as Jordan had pointed out, this was business. Nothing personal. When they were at the office he had no choice but to talk to him.

"Have you got a minute?" Jordan asked.

Nathan gestured him inside.

"So, the board meeting is this afternoon," Jordan said, as if Nathan wasn't already well aware of that fact.

"So it is," he said.

"You should know that I had planned to go to the board and tell them about you and Ana."

"I figured as much."

"Well, I changed my mind. I'm not going to do it."

"Am I supposed to thank you?"

"No. I just thought you would want to know."

"It wouldn't matter now anyway. We split up a week ago."

He looked truly taken aback. "You split up? Why?"

"What difference does it make?"

"Nathan, if it's because of what I said—"

"When you insinuated the woman I love is a slut?"

Jordan actually looked remorseful. "I was just trying to ruffle your feathers. I didn't think you would take me seriously."

"Then you'll be relieved to know that it has nothing to do with that."

"Damn, I'm sorry it didn't work out. What about Max?"

"I'm not seeing Max either."

"*What?* Is she keeping him from you?"

"It was my own choice."

"Are you crazy? You love that kid. And he adores you. I've never seen you so happy."

"It's the only way I can keep them safe."

"From what?"

"Me. Like you said, I'm just like *him*."

He rolled his eyes. "Nathan, those were just words said in the heat of the moment. I was trying to piss you off, *trying* to make you hit me."

Huh? "You wanted me to hit you?"

"Because I knew it would make you feel lousy when you did. Because…" He drew in a deep breath and blew it out. "Hell, I don't know. Maybe it's the enormous chip I've been carrying around on my shoulder for the past twenty or so years."

"You *resent* me. Jordan, I took—"

"You took care of me, I know. You defended me against the whole damned world. Did it ever occur to you to let me defend myself or, instead of fighting my battles for me, teaching *me* how to fight them? Maybe I didn't need you to be my damned savior."

His words stunned Nathan. All these years he assumed he was doing his brother a favor by protecting him. Had he actually done more harm than good? "I guess, since I was older, I considered it my responsibility to take care of you."

"Do you have any idea how guilty I used to feel when Dad would whale on you for something I did? After a while I started to resent you for it, for thinking I was too weak to take care of myself. Then it got to the point when I actually enjoyed getting you in trouble, watching you take the knocks for things I did. I wanted you to feel as weak and as small as I did."

"Jordan, I was only trying to help. I had no idea I was making you feel that way."

Jordan shrugged. "So, now you know. And this thing with Ana and Max, you don't want to screw the pooch on this one. You'll regret it for the rest of your life."

"I would regret it a lot more if I hurt them."

"You're not going to hurt them. Not physically anyway. Over the years I've given you a hundred reasons to clean my clock, and look how long it took for you to actually take a swing at me. And the expression on your face afterward..." Jordan laughed and shook his head. "You looked like you backed over a puppy with your car. That alone was worth the sore jaw."

Nathan grinned for the first time in a week. "I really looked that bad?"

"It was freaking awesome. And it astounds me that after all the years, and all the bullshit, you don't hate my guts. No matter how hard I push you, how big of a jerk I am, you're still there for me. If I called you at 3:00 a.m. from some bar, too wasted to drive, and said I needed a ride, you would drop everything and pick me up." He paused, then said, "Which I guess in a way makes *you* the weak one, not me."

"Because if I called you for a ride in the middle of the night...?"

"I'd tell you to call a damn cab, then I'd roll over and go back to sleep."

No, he wouldn't. Nathan didn't know how he knew. He just did. If Jordan didn't care about him, they wouldn't be having this conversation. Maybe there was hope for them yet.

"Don't think this changes anything," Jordan said.

"When it comes to the CEO position I'm going to leave you in the dust. Then I'll be your boss. Think how much fun that will be."

"You have to get through me first."

Jordan grinned, turned and walked out of Nathan's office.

Nathan sat there for a minute, a little stunned, trying to process what had just happened, what had been resolved, and trying to figure out what it meant, but it felt as if the walls were closing in on him. He needed to get out of here. He needed fresh air, a chance to clear his head and really think.

He grabbed his coat and headed out of his office, telling his secretary to cancel all his appointments and that he would be back later that day.

Maybe. The truth was, he didn't know where he was going or how long he would be there. The way he was feeling, he could get in the car, pick a direction and never look back.

Instead, after driving in circles for a while, he found himself in the last place he'd ever expected to be. His father's house.

# Sixteen

The Everette family estate looked exactly as it had the last time Nathan was there ten years ago, and ten years before that. In his entire life he didn't think it had changed much.

Maybe that should have been a comfort, but it wasn't.

He had no idea why he was here or what he planned to do, but suddenly he was out of the car and walking up to the porch. It was as if he was following some predetermined flight plan he had absolutely no control over.

He climbed the front steps and stopped at the door, raising his hand to knock. Then he dropped it back down to his side.

What the hell was he doing? There was a damned good reason he'd spent the last ten years avoiding this place. Avoiding his father. This wouldn't solve anything.

He turned to leave, stopping as his foot hit the first step, unable to go any farther. Damn it. Somehow he knew that until he did this, until he faced his father, he wouldn't be able to move on with his life. He would be caught in a perpetual cycle of self-doubt from which he might never break free. He needed to do this for himself, and for Max.

Before he could change his mind, he walked back to the door and rapped hard. Besides, what were the odds that he would be home at two in the afternoon anyway?

The housekeeper opened the door. When she saw who was standing there, she slapped a hand to her bosom, which along with her middle seemed to have expanded over the years, and her hair was more silver than the pale blond it used to be. "Nathan! My goodness, it's been years!"

"Hi, Sylvia. Is my father by any chance home?"

"As a matter of fact he is. He's just getting over a cold, so he's working from home today."

Dumb fricking luck. "Can you tell him I'm here?"

"Of course! Come on inside. Can I take your coat?"

"I can't stay long."

"Well, I'll go get him then."

She hurried off in the direction of the study while Nathan looked around. Unlike the outside, someone had given the interior a major overhaul. The gaudy and nauseating pastels his mother had been so fond of had been replaced with a more Southwestern feel. Probably one of his father's multiple wives made the change.

"Nathan! What a surprise!"

He turned to see his father walking toward him, and blinked with surprise. For some reason he expected him to look exactly as he had the last time he'd seen him. And though only ten years had passed it looked as though he had aged double that. His hair was more salt than pepper and his face was a roadmap of lines and wrinkles. He was the same height he'd always been, but he seemed smaller somehow, a scaled-down version of his former self. In slacks, a button-down plaid shirt and a pullover sweater, he looked more like Mister Rogers than the monster Nathan remembered.

"Hi, Dad."

"I would shake your hand but I'm just getting over a terrible cold. I wouldn't want to risk passing my germs along to you."

"I appreciate that." Besides, he wasn't here to exchange pleasantries.

"Why don't we sit in my study? Can I get you a drink?"

"I can't stay long."

"Your brother tells me you're both competing for the CEO position at Western Oil."

That shouldn't have raised his hackles, but it did. "I didn't come here to talk about Jordan," he snapped.

His father shrank back visibly. He nodded and stuck his hands in his pants pockets. "Okay, what did you come here for?"

He honestly had no clue. "This was a bad idea," he said. "I'm sorry to have bothered you."

He turned to leave, and got to the door before he realized that he couldn't go, not until he had some answers. He turned back to his father. "I have a son."

His father blinked with surprise. "I—I didn't know. How old is he?"

"Nine months. His name is Max."

"Congratulations."

"He's a great kid. He looks a lot like me, but he has his mother's eyes. And he has the Everette birthmark." A ball of emotion rolled up into his throat. "He's beautiful and smart and I love him more than life itself, and I'm probably never going to see him again."

"Why?"

"Because I'm so damned afraid that I'm going to do to him what you did to me." He hadn't expected to blurt that out, and clearly his father hadn't, either. There was nothing like getting right to the point.

"Why don't you come in and sit down?" his father said.

"I don't want to sit down. I just want to know why. Why did you do it? Tell me why so I can figure out how to be different."

"Not a day goes by that I don't regret the way I treated you and your brother. I know I wasn't a great father."

"That does not help me."

His father shrugged. "I guess…it was the way I was raised. It's all I knew."

Great. So, it was some twisted family tradition. That was just swell. "So in other words, I'm screwed."

He sighed and shook his head. "*No.* You have a choice. Just like I did. I chose not to change. I spent twenty miserable years with a woman I loved more than life itself, and all she wanted from me was my name and as much of my money as she could get her greedy hands on. I was bitter and heartbroken, and instead of taking it out on the person who deserved it, I took it out on my kids."

"You actually *loved* her?" Somehow he found that hard to believe. She was just so…unlovable. Stunningly beautiful, yes, but cold and selfish.

"Of course I loved her. Why did you think I married her?"

"Because she was pregnant."

"She didn't find out she was pregnant until after we were engaged. Almost two months, if memory serves."

Nathan shook his head. "That can't be right. I heard grandmother and Aunt Caroline talking when I was a kid. They said you *had* to get married."

"Your grandmother never liked your mom. She thought she was beneath the Everette name. She was furious when she found out that I proposed. I think she had herself convinced that I would come to my senses and break the engagement, so when your mom got pregnant, I guess in her own twisted way, your grandmother probably thought we *had* to get married."

Nathan was beginning to think that everything he knew about his life was wrong. Or at the very least grossly misinterpreted. There was only one thing that didn't make sense...

"You said it's the way you were raised, but didn't your father die when you were four years old?"

"I don't really remember him, but as far as I know, my father never laid a hand on me."

It took a second for the meaning of his words to sink in. "Are you saying Grandmother..."

"She looked harmless, but that woman was mean as a snake."

Damn. It was bad enough for a boy to be bullied by his father, but coming from his mother it had to be even more humiliating and degrading. Then to be married to a woman he loved who didn't love him back. Picking on his sons, who were too young to defend themselves, must have made him feel empowered.

"Son, the bottom line is that your grandmother was a very unhappy person, and so was I. I was a miserable excuse for a father. And nowhere does it say that you're destined to be just like me. You can be whatever kind of father you want to be. *You* make the choice."

If it was his choice, then he *chose* to be different. And if he made mistakes, they would be his own, and hopefully he would learn from them along the way.

"I have to go," he told his father.

He nodded, but he looked...sad. And for a second Nathan actually felt sorry for him. Which beat the hell out of hating him.

"Maybe you could stop by again sometime," he said. "I don't know if your brother told you, but I'm getting married. *Again*."

"He mentioned it."

He shrugged. "Who knows, maybe this one will stick."

"Maybe I could bring Max by to see you some time."

"Does that mean you will be seeing him again?"

If Ana would let him. And even if she didn't, being in his son's life was something he considered worth fighting for.

But before he fought that battle, he had a board meeting to crash.

"Okay," Beth said, pressing the End button on her cell phone and jotting down a date and time in her daily planner. She set the book on the coffee table and sank back into the couch. "I have an appointment with the marriage counselor next Monday at 7:00 p.m. I made it later just in case Leo decides to come with me."

But they both knew he wouldn't. At least not yet. After finding a hotel room charge on Leo's credit card bill, from two days *after* New Year's, Beth finally took a stand. She insisted they go into counseling, and when he refused, she decided to go alone.

It was definitely a start.

Ana put her hand on Beth's arm and gave it a squeeze. "I'm very proud of you. This is a huge step."

"One that I wish my husband was making with me. But if he doesn't love me enough to try to save our marriage, maybe it isn't worth saving." Tears welled in her eyes, but she took a deep breath and blinked them back. "But I'm going to get through it." She put her hand over Ana's. "We both are."

Yeah, except Nathan did love her, and he loved Max,

and he wanted to be with them, but he was just being a big idiot. And she was an idiot for believing him when he said he wouldn't hurt her. But never again. He'd had his chance and he blew it. A few days ago she might have taken him back. She had still been in the mourning stage, crying every time she thought about him, but now she was angry—and boy, was she *angry*—and if he dared show up at her door, she was going to be the one gunning to "hurt" someone.

"I should probably pick Piper up from the babysitter's and get home to make dinner," Beth said. "Or better yet, maybe I'll just grab something on the way home. Maybe Thai or sushi, Leo's least favorites."

The doorbell rang and Ana's heart dropped into her knees. The way it had every time the doorbell rang this past week. But it wasn't going to be Nathan. It never was. She didn't want to see him even if it was, but it was just an automatic reaction, like Pavlov's dog.

"I better get that," she said, pushing herself up from the couch, deliberately not looking out the window before she pulled the door open.

She sucked in a surprised breath when she saw Nathan standing on her porch. *Way to play it cool, Ana. Great job.*

"Hi," he said, and her heart dropped from her knees and landed in the balls of her feet. He looked *good*. So good that for a second she forgot to be angry. She very nearly launched herself at him.

"I'm very mad at you," she said, more to remind herself than to warn him.

"I just want to talk," he said, and the deep rumble of his voice danced across her nerve endings, making her shiver.

*Whatever you do, just stay mad. Do not throw yourself into his arms.*

"I have company over right now," she said.

"And I was just leaving," Beth said from behind her.

She turned to Beth and glared at her. Traitor.

Beth pulled her coat on and kissed Ana's cheek. "I'll call you tomorrow." As she stepped down to the porch beside Nathan she looked up at him and said, "Hurt her again and I will take you out."

Nathan's brows rose a fraction, and she could swear she saw the hint of a smile. What did he have to smile about? She hoped he wasn't here thinking he was going to get her back. Because that was not going to happen.

He stepped inside and took off his coat. He was still dressed for work. "Is Max here?"

She shook her head. "He's at Jenny's for a play date."

"That's good. We can talk without any distractions."

"Who says I want to talk?"

"Well, you let me in, didn't you?"

Not a smart move on her part. Because maybe she wasn't quite as mad as she'd thought.

"Can we go sit down?" he asked.

That would be a bad idea. She wanted him close to the door so she could shove him out on a moment's notice if she got any funny ideas. Or if he did. "I'm comfortable right here."

He shrugged and said, "Okay."

"So, what did you want to talk about?"

"I have had an interesting day."

"Oh yeah? And why should I care?"

"My brother and I had a heart-to-heart talk today. I think we may have resolved a few things."

"That's good, I guess. Although I still wouldn't trust him."

"And I went to see my dad."

Whoa. She definitely hadn't expected him to say that. "Why?"

"I'm not sure. I went out for a drive, and I just ended up there. Maybe subconsciously I figured that when you have a problem to solve, it's best to go to the source. He was my source."

She folded her arms and against her better judgement asked, "How did that go?"

"It was…enlightening. It would seem that my dad actually loved my mom, and when he proposed to her, she was in fact not pregnant."

"Oh."

"He loved her so much that he stayed married to her, even though he knew she only wanted his money. And he was miserably unhappy."

"That's kinda sad."

"That's the difference between him and me, I guess. I wasn't unhappy. At least, not until I screwed everything up. Before that, I was really, really happy."

Yeah, so was she. But it was *over*.

She inched closer to the door. If he kept this up, he was out of here. Or maybe she should just run.

"I think I wanted you to fix me," he said. "I just needed to figure out that the only person who can fix me is *me*."

If she yanked the door open, grabbed his sleeve and tugged she could probably muscle him onto the porch. "Are you saying you're *fixed* now?"

"I'm saying that I've isolated the problem, and though I'm not one hundred percent there, I'm definitely a work in progress. But there is a problem."

Well that was good, because she needed a problem or two to firm up her resolve. "What problem?"

"I'm in love with you, and I miss my son, and without the two of you in my life permanently, I don't think I can be happy."

*Don't even think about it. You are not giving him another chance.* She was inches from the doorknob...

"I went before the board today."

"What for?"

"To tell them about you and Max. I assured them that being married to a Birch was not going to diminish my loyalty to Western Oil. I don't know if they believed me, but they didn't take me out of the running. I guess time will tell."

"Nathan, why did you do that?"

"Because it was wrong of me to try to hide you. Max is my son. Keeping his existence a secret is tantamount to saying that I'm ashamed of him. And I'm not. I love him and I'm proud of him and I want everyone to know that. And I want them to know that I love his mother, and I want to spend the rest of my life loving her." He reached up and touched her cheek. "And *she* is the most important thing to me. Not the job."

She had waited an awfully long time for someone to feel that way about her. To put her first. "You know, you're making it really hard for me to stay mad at you."

He grinned. "That's sort of the point, since I could really use one more chance."

Like she had any hope of resisting him now. She threw her arms around him and hugged him hard. "One more. But if you screw up this time, I swear I'm siccing Beth on you."

"This time you're definitely stuck with me." He wrapped his arms around her, held her close. "I missed you. And Max. This has been the most miserable week of my life."

"Mine too." But she was good now. Really, really good.

"I love you, Ana."

"I love you, too. Why don't I go get Max? He's going to be so happy to see you."

"Wait. Before you do, there's one more thing we have to talk about."

His face was so serious, her heart plunged. "What?"

He reached into his jacket pocket and pulled something out. It took her a second to realize that it was a small velvet box. A *ring* box. Then he actually dropped down on one knee.

*Oh my God.* Her heart was beating so hard she thought for sure it would break right through her chest.

He opened the box, and inside was a diamond solitaire ring. It was so beautiful it took her breath away. "Ana, would you do me the honor of being my wife?"

She had fantasized about this day since she was a little girl but could never have imagined how truly special it would be. She was getting everything she ever wanted. That and so much more.

"Yes I will, Nathan," she said, through a sheen of tears—happy ones this time—and with a grin, he slipped the ring on her finger.

\* \* \* \* \*

# COMING NEXT MONTH

## Available September 13, 2011

# REQUEST YOUR FREE BOOKS!

## 2 FREE NOVELS PLUS 2 FREE GIFTS!

### ALWAYS POWERFUL, PASSIONATE AND PROVOCATIVE

**YES!** Please send me 2 FREE Harlequin Desire® novels and my 2 FREE gifts (gifts are worth about $10). After receiving them, if I don't wish to receive any more books, I can return the shipping statement marked "cancel." If I don't cancel, I will receive 6 brand-new novels every month and be billed just $4.30 per book in the U.S. or $4.99 per book in Canada. That's a saving of at least 14% off the cover price! It's quite a bargain! Shipping and handling is just 50¢ per book in the U.S. and 75¢ per book in Canada.* I understand that accepting the 2 free books and gifts places me under no obligation to buy anything. I can always return a shipment and cancel at any time. Even if I never buy another book, the two free books and gifts are mine to keep forever.

225/326 HDN FEF3

Name _____ (PLEASE PRINT) _____

Address _____ Apt. # _____

City _____ State/Prov. _____ Zip/Postal Code _____

Signature (if under 18, a parent or guardian must sign)

### Mail to the **Reader Service:**

**IN U.S.A.:** P.O. Box 1867, Buffalo, NY 14240-1867
**IN CANADA:** P.O. Box 609, Fort Erie, Ontario  L2A 5X3

Not valid for current subscribers to Harlequin Desire books.

**Want to try two free books from another line?**
**Call 1-800-873-8635 or visit www.ReaderService.com.**

* Terms and prices subject to change without notice. Prices do not include applicable taxes. Sales tax applicable in N.Y. Canadian residents will be charged applicable taxes. Offer not valid in Quebec. This offer is limited to one order per household. All orders subject to credit approval. Credit or debit balances in a customer's account(s) may be offset by any other outstanding balance owed by or to the customer. Please allow 4 to 6 weeks for delivery. Offer available while quantities last.

**Your Privacy**—The Reader Service is committed to protecting your privacy. Our Privacy Policy is available online at www.ReaderService.com or upon request from the Reader Service.

We make a portion of our mailing list available to reputable third parties that offer products we believe may interest you. If you prefer that we not exchange your name with third parties, or if you wish to clarify or modify your communication preferences, please visit us at www.ReaderService.com/consumerschoice or write to us at Reader Service Preference Service, P.O. Box 9062, Buffalo, NY 14269. Include your complete name and address.

HDES11B

New York Times *and* USA TODAY *bestselling author*
*Maya Banks presents a brand-new miniseries*

PREGNANCY & PASSION

*When four irresistible tycoons face
the consequences of temptation.*

*Book 1—ENTICED BY HIS FORGOTTEN LOVER*

*Available September 2011 from Harlequin® Desire®!*

Rafael de Luca had been in bad situations before. A crowded ballroom could never make him sweat.

These people would never know that he had no memory of any of them.

He surveyed the party with grim tolerance, searching for the source of his unease.

At first his gaze flickered past her, but he yanked his attention back to a woman across the room. Her stare bored holes through him. Unflinching and steady, even when his eyes locked with hers.

Petite, even in heels, she had a creamy olive complexion. A wealth of inky-black curls cascaded over her shoulders and her eyes were equally dark.

She looked at him as if she'd already judged him and found him lacking. He'd never seen her before in his life. Or had he?

He cursed the gaping hole in his memory. He'd been diagnosed with selective amnesia after his accident four months ago. Which seemed like complete and utter bull. No one got amnesia except hysterical women in bad soap operas.

With a smile, he disengaged himself from the group

around him and made his way to the mystery woman.

She wasn't coy. She stared straight at him as he approached, her chin thrust upward in defiance.

"Excuse me, but have we met?" he asked in his smoothest voice.

His gaze moved over the generous swell of her breasts pushed up by the empire waist of her black cocktail dress.

When he glanced back up at her face, he saw fury in her eyes.

"Have we *met?*" Her voice was barely a whisper, but he felt each word like the crack of a whip.

Before he could process her response, she nailed him with a right hook. He stumbled back, holding his nose.

One of his guards stepped between Rafe and the woman, accidentally sending her to one knee. Her hand flew to the folds of her dress.

It was then, as she cupped her belly, that the realization hit him. She was pregnant.

Her eyes flashing, she turned and ran down the marble hallway.

Rafael ran after her. He burst from the hotel lobby, and saw two shoes sparkling in the moonlight, twinkling at him.

He blew out his breath in frustration and then shoved the pair of sparkly, ultrafeminine heels at his head of security.

"Find the woman who wore these shoes."

*Will Rafael find his mystery woman?*
*Find out in Maya Banks's passionate new novel*
*ENTICED BY HIS FORGOTTEN LOVER*
*Available September 2011 from Harlequin® Desire®!*

# Harlequin *Desire*

ALWAYS POWERFUL, PASSIONATE AND PROVOCATIVE.

**NEW YORK TIMES AND USA TODAY
BESTSELLING AUTHOR**

# MAYA BANKS

**BRINGS YOU THE FIRST STORY
IN A BRAND-NEW MINISERIES**

## PASSION & PREGNANCY
*When irresistible tycoons
face the consequences of temptation.*

# ENTICED BY HIS
# FORGOTTEN LOVER

A bout of amnesia…a mysterious woman
he can't resist…a pregnancy shocker.

When Rafael de Luca's memory comes
crashing back, it will change everything.

*Available September
wherever books are sold.*